Their Safe Landing
Book 1
The Rayne Falls Ranch Collection

Sinful Grace

ISBN-1: 978-1-7349328-0-5

Their Safe Landing

Dear Reader,

I hope you enjoy this book, as it's my first book not only being published but in this series. I would like to dedicate this book to my husband, who even though he has not read this book, pushed me to publish it knowing how important this was to me. I would also like to give recognition to the friends and authors I have had the pleasure of getting to know from the writer's espresso book group. Both women who run the group are great motivators and knowledgeable in their experiences within this process.

A bit about myself: I am a married mother of four. I work with several rescues both in the states and overseas. I work from home, yes with all my kids; as a medical professional, and have a great understanding of imagination. Romance is not only what I write about but am passionate about. There is an art in the languages of love, affection, compassion, kink, erotica, and romance in general. I find all of it to be enchanting and I hope you can see some of that within my work.

When I am not working, corralling kids, or writing, I am trying to play with animals or crafting. I am not only artsy in writing but other projects too. I cannot sit still.

Within this book, you will find that the main characters face a conflict. I know at some point in our lives we all face different conflicts and sometimes we find love within the face of those conflicts. Knowing who we can count on is the main draw to any relationship and it is my wish that you find yourself connecting to the characters in this book like I did.

Finally, if you feel you are in a bad situation, please reach out to someone. Your local authorities are a place to start but sometimes that is not always an option. If you feel uncomfortable doing so, please reach out to a hotline. One hotline is the National Domestic Abuse Hotline: 1-800-799-7233 (www.thehotline.org). The National Sexual Abuse Hotline: 1-800-656-4673. Or also reach out to www.childhelp.org if you need help with children. Please know there are resources to help if you need it. Always stay safe my readers. You are all important.

If you wish to check out more of my work, contact me, or provide feedback, please visit:

www.gt-publishing.com

https://www.facebook.com/SinfulGraceRomanceAuthor/

https://www.facebook.com/georgia.grace.50702

https://writersespresso.com

https://writersespresso.com/Sinful-Grace

Twitter: @Sinful_Grace

Instagram: Sinful_Grace

Remember,
You can't have history without a story in it!

Sinful Grace

Quod nocet, saepe docet.

What harms, often teaches,

- Latin proverb

Chapter 1

An autumn breeze swept in the driver's side window to flow through her honey auburn hair. Making her tear-streaked face turn chilled. Annette didn't notice that it had gotten a bit colder and darker within the last hour of driving. In fact, she barely noticed that she had been crying. The only thing she felt was the latest bruise on her arm where she had been grabbed and dragged across her hotel room floor; along with the already purplish eye she had been given for her efforts to get away.

But she did get away, and that is what she focused on now. Running. She was faced with it no matter where she went. Only lately it has been more frequent. The last place she just fled from she had only been there for three days. Three days and he found her! How did he do it so quickly?

A bump in the road brought her back to the present. Glancing in her rearview to check on her dozing daughter, she sighed. It was close this time. He hadn't been able to get past her to the closet where her daughter was hiding. Oh, he tried to get to her. Having physical proof of his efforts. Although Annette knew from previous attacks that it could get much worse had he lost his full temper. When he completely goes off there is no telling exactly what he would do. The situation could become extremely dangerous. A few years ago, he had gotten so mad that he blacked out. Even after numerous hospital visits and medications she still felt the broken bones as if it was yesterday.

A soft snore from her daughter put a smile on her face. She was the one thing that she had gotten right. That little girl was the only reason for pushing on and not giving up. After everything they have been put through, she will not lay down and just take it anymore. Giving the steering wheel a smack to emphasize her resolve.

Growling from her stomach reminded her that neither of them had eaten. A swift glance at the clock proved that it had been hours since they had a meal and her stomach was not about to let her get away with it. Inwardly groaning, she got off at the next exit. Checking all her mirrors to make sure no one was following close behind her before pulling out onto the tight two-lane road. She knew that daylight would only enhance her chances of being found, but she quietly wished she had some since it was pitch black and she didn't know where she was. A bright neon sign for a dinner caught her eye about two miles up the road.

Pulling into the parking lot and stopping the car didn't change the numbness that still welled within her. The bright blue and orange neon sign saying 'Mickey's' didn't really fit with her mood at all but she could smell the food from her window and the rumbling from her stomach began to increase. Rolling up the window she climbed out of her old sedan. Grabbing a sweater to hide her torn shirt and bruises on her arms, hoping that no one would notice her right eye.

After taking a few breaths to make sure she wasn't going to cry anymore she forced a smile to her face and opened the rear door. "Sweetie", a little nudge "Honey, it's time to eat." She heard a yawn. A small arm shot up as she stretched. After rubbing her eyes, she turned her head to look at her mother.

"Mommy?" She said in a soft whisper.

"Yes baby, it's me. You need to wake up. Are you hungry?" softly cooing the words to rouse her from her sleep.

"I'm tired, Mommy." More eye rubbing. Her eyes a bit swollen still from all the crying she had done earlier. "Do we have to eat?" She began to lay back again. "Yes, baby. We need to get up now. Come on." Unbuckling her car seat and lifting her out proved to be too much for her injured arm. Tears pooled in her eyes but she didn't allow for them to fall. Her daughter laying her cheek on her shoulder gave her the comfort she needed to walk inside.

The musty smell greeted her as she pulled the door open. The overhead bell jingling was the only sound she heard as the place fell to a queasy silence. Everyone held her in their gaze, questioning her. The outsider. Annette met some of their eyes with her own stare. Nudging her daughter up a bit higher onto her shoulder, she walked further into the room. Feeling the patrons' eyes following her.

The waitress broke her stride by stepping in front of her. Her southern accent comforting her slightly. "Hullo ma'am. Can I get you a seat?" Annette took in the light frosty blue uniform. The dress came below her knees and had a white apron layover. It looked a bit out of place with her bright pink name badge and dark brown glasses, but she still gave a reassuring feel with the big smile and curly brown hair.
Taking a second to read her name badge with a bit of difficulty from the sheer brightness of it, "Sam. Thank you." Forcing as good a smile as she could muster, with not much success.

"Well alright then. Will you be needing a high chair?" Sam started pulling out menus and placemats as she waited for a response.

"No thank you."

Nodding she motioned for her to follow with a wave of her wrist. The conversation began stirring again and Annette overheard that some of it were people questioning her. Heading no mind to the endless chatter going on around her she followed the young girl and took the booth offered to her. Giving a groan of relief as the child was let off of her shoulder onto the semi torn red seat. She turned around to see the girl intently watching her.

"You're not from around, here are you?" The girl seemed to take note of her face but said nothing. Just a knowing glance and then another smile; a little less chipper this time.

"No just passing through I suppose." Annette said.

Annette lifted up her sleeping daughter's head to rest upon her lap as she slid into the booth. After brushing her hair from her little face, she placed a kiss on her forehead. Resuming where she left off in her conversation, "Unless you know of a hotel near here where we can get some rest?"

"Well there is a motel about ten miles up the road, but I believe they are shut down due to repairs." A frown showed for an instant and then it was gone. Replaced yet again by one of her white smiles.

"Oh, okay. Thank you anyway." Not realizing how much she had been hoping for a room until she heard the disappointment in her own voice.

"What would you like to drink?" Sam's voice getting a bit louder as she pulled out a pen and paper.

"Just water for me, and if you could get some milk for her."

"Sure Hun, I'll be right back with those." And without even writing anything down, she placed the pad and pen back into her apron; turned and left.

All the nerves in her body were on edge, her muscles tense and her senses on alert. Surveying the room, she took note of the exits, the people mingling around in seats and at the counter. She noticed she was placed in a booth with no windows and near the bathrooms. Now she doubted it was done intentionally but none the less it was a plus for her. She would be less noticed if he were to come looking for her in here.

The dinner reminded her of some she had seen when she was younger. The smell and the wear on the place are telltale signs that it has not only been here for a while but has seen better days. Some of the windows have that dark film, while others were clear. The seats are worn down and torn in places. The tabletop has that yellow vinyl that is cracked and bubbled in places.

The weather outside seemed to get even darker if it was possible. Mimicking her mood and only amplifying it when it started to pour down hard against the metal roof. The sound creating harsh echoes inside, which in turn made everyone have to speak even louder to be heard.

The drinks arrived with a thud on the table that stirred her daughter awake. Shooting straight up and wiping her eyes again. Sam apologized while wiping up the tiny spill with a napkin. Annette tried to reassure her it was okay and she didn't have to trouble herself, but she took the glass back and went to get another one. Commenting over her shoulder she'll be back to place her order in a second.

She felt so much love for this little girl next to her and every day she could not fathom her life without her. A shooting pain of fear from earlier came rushing back. She rubbed her daughters back to reassure herself that she really was here and no physical harm had come to her.

Turning at the sound of the doorbell with her heart in her throat she almost expected it to be him. Only when she noticed the elderly lady taking off her rain-soaked coat did she allow for her body to relax back into the seat. The waitress called out to the lady as she passed her. "Carolynn I'll be with you to take your order in a minute. Go sit down wherever you like."

The elderly lady said a short thank you and waved to a few of the people sitting at the counter before moving to take a seat in the booth behind Annette. Annette felt the seat lean more into her from behind as she slid fully in. This would normally have bothered her but she decided this would serve as more cover for her if she needed it.

"Here we go Hun. Sorry again for making a mess. Oh, hello there Darling, and who might you be?" Sam bending over a bit to look into her daughters' eyes. Perking up and sitting on her knees, as her daughter always did when she had an audience, she grabbed at her mother's arm.

"This is my mommy!" Pulling on her arm to make a point. "I'm not supposed to talk to strangers, Mommy said so." Her daughter replied with more enthusiasm than was necessary. Annette turned and smiled at Sam whose smile never faltered but got only more endearing with the softness in her eyes.

"And she would be right to tell you that Darlin."

Turning to face her daughter, Annette gave a nod of her head, "it's okay baby, you can tell her."

"Oh, if she doesn't want to it's okay. No harm done." Sam tried to reassure her.

"Sure Mom?" And with another nod, her daughter sat up straight and stuck out her hand, "I'm Holly."

This seemed to surprise Sam as much as it did her, but Sam recovered quickly. Grabbing her hand and lightly shaking it she said, "Well nice to meet you. My name is Sam."

Annette lifted up the menu after her daughter took her hand back and started drinking her milk. Sam took this as her queue to grab in her apron again but Annette stopped her.

"All we are going to get is some scrambled eggs." Before she could question for anything else Annette handed over the menu and began sipping from her water. Sam turned and left without another word. Holly didn't make a sound until she started getting bored after finishing her glass.

"Mommy where are we?" She said so softly Annette had to strain a little to hear it.

Taking a few seconds to think she replied, "A dinner baby. I believe it's called Mike's?"

A comforting voice came from behind correcting her, almost startling her enough to scream. "Mickey's is the name I believe you mean."

Annette put her hand to her chest and spun around. She was greeted by light silver-colored eyes.

Realizing the woman was also staring back at her, she momentarily lost her speech. The woman's cheeks got a flush of color to them. "Sorry Dear, didn't mean to startle you. Names Carolann but everyone calls me Carolynn. Don't quite know why."

Clearing her throat to make sure she wouldn't squeak when she finally spoke, she attempted to get out some words. "It's fine, just didn't expect it." Feeling as though her voice sounded more solid to her she went on, "My name is Annette. And this here is Holly."

Carolynn turned her gaze to her daughter next to her and produced a gentle smile. "Well nice to meet you both. You staying in Montana long?"

Annette began to shake her head as their food arrived. Sam placed their plates out in front of them with new drinks. Saying thank you and excusing herself from the conversation she began to feed her daughter.

The hushed chatter of Sam talking to Carolynn behind her helped her to focus her mind. It is the last thing that she wanted to do but needed to be done. Lights flickering and dimming in the room were proof of the storm capping. Wind so strong you hear the whooshing against the windows. It was as if Mother Nature was fighting with herself.

What was she going to do next? Where were they going to stay? She never even called the police after this last escape because what was the point? It never helped. Even if they found him and took him, he always found his way back to her. The restraining order she had gotten didn't even deter him. It was a never-ending cycle. No. She was not going to call the police. Instead, she was going to keep her mouth shut this time. Try to hide it as much as possible. She was unsure if it would make a difference but it would be a different route she hadn't tried yet. And at this point, she was starting to feel the exhaustion from being so wound up. She knew she couldn't do this forever. Her daughter would need to start school soon and then what?

She didn't want her growing up on the run, or completely out of school. She wanted stability for Holly. Family is so precious and even though Annette had none left except her daughter she could build off of community, that is if she ever stayed long enough in one place.

Sorrow and regret had no place in her consciousness right now. She needed to maintain a sense of hardness if she was going to get out from under this. As if sensing something, the elderly lady behind her tapped her on the shoulder and asked if she was alright. Responding with a nod was apparently not satisfying. Carolynn was obviously not buying it. However, she was also polite enough not to comment. Sam came by again to refill their cups and left to make her rounds around the room.

Carolynn made idle conversation about the weather and work on her farm. Annette trying to pay attention but feeling the normal pullback in her mind. An impulse she has when trying not to get attached to people. It became second nature to her and at this point, it happened involuntarily.

Holly began pulling on her sleeve to tell her she was done with her food. "I'm tired Mommy." Emphasizing this with her own tiny yawn.

"Oh my. I do believe the little Dear needs her rest."

"Yes, she does." Annette pulled her daughter onto her lap. Her own scrambled eggs, cold and forgotten on the table. Just as well since she wasn't hungry anymore with the knots in her stomach. "Honey, you can nap in the car okay? We still have a lot of driving left to do." Holly just snuggled closer to her chest and began to nod off.

"A lot of driving? My, but you look quite tired yourself." Carolynn questioning her with her eyes. "Where you headed to Dearie?"

Annette took a few seconds before she answered to think about what she was going to say. Staling a bit longer by kissing her daughter's forehead. "I'm not quite sure yet as to my designation,"
She decided a bit of the truth wouldn't hurt. "I'm still looking for a place to stay for the night, but I heard the Motel was closed."

Carolynn seemed to take in every word. She even obviously took in her appearance. Annette could tell the other woman had a storm going on in her own mind. Hearing the door again Annette Jumped a bit, stirring her daughter. Carolynn missed nothing. She looked at the door and turned back to her. Concern written on her face.

"Are you alright? You seem a bit tense."

The pounding in her ears began to recede as she realized it wasn't him. Her daughter seemed to have gone back to sleep against her as well. Remembering the other woman had asked her a question she turned her gaze back to her. Carolynn began clicking her tongue as she waited for her answer.

"Sorry. Yes, I am okay. I think I am a bit more tired then I realized." She was hoping the other woman would not notice the falseness to her words since the words spilled out of her mouth in a rush. Forcing a smile to her face, even if it was a broken one, seemed to ease the other lady as well.

The lady ran her fingers through her salt and pepper hair and fidgeted around in her purse for something. She pulled out some keys and laid a few bills on the table. "Well, it seems to me that if you're as tired as all that, then you shouldn't be driving around in the middle of the night. Especially without knowing where you are and with a little one in the back seat." She held up her hand as Annette began to protest. "Don't sass me, Dear. I know your plum tuckered out. I can see it all over you."

Satisfied she was not going to get an argument she went on, "Now I couldn't in my right mind allow for you to go driving off tonight in the state you're in. Being as I have a conscious and such. So, humor an old lady. You can stay at my house and in the morning my grandson will bring you back to your car." Seeing Annette begin to shake her head Carolynn began to cluck her tongue again. "Don't make me have to have Sam lock the doors so you can't leave."

She wasn't entirely sure the woman had meant it or not. Normally she would just assume she was pulling her leg but seeing the firm set of the other woman's mouth she was betting she wasn't bluffing. Reluctantly she nodded her head yes and stood up with her daughter still wrapped tightly within her arms. She turned to pay Sam, who was already picking up her plates as though she had been counting on this to happen.

"No, ma'am. Put your money back. It's on the house on account of you being new around here and all. Besides you barely ate anything." She gave another one of her smiles, lightly patted her arm and cleaned the table.

Unaccustomed to being taken care of, she wasn't sure of the weird feelings inside her. Instead of dwelling on it, plus feeling the heaviness of her daughter on her injured arm, she followed Carolynn out the door.

The rain didn't stop entirely but came down in little spurts. Just enough to keep the ground damp but nothing to completely cool off the humidity outside. Fog was beginning to show in the air around them but just ever so faintly. She noticed the big red truck the woman walked up to and almost laughed out loud. It did not suit her at all. She looked even more fragile and tiny next to it.

"Well Dearie if you need anything from your car, I suggest you get it now, cuz you won't be back till morning."

"I don't really have that much, but I should probably get her car seat."

Again, echoed the sound of her clucking her tongue. Seemingly in disapproval. "I'll hold the little one for ya. Don't you have any clothes you'll be needing?"

Slipping her daughter out of her arms and turning to go fetch the seat she said, "No. No clothes."

Carolynn not only had to lean in a bit to hear her since she spoke so softly, but she also didn't comment. Annette took this time to get the car seat situated in the bigger vehicle in between the two women and strapped her in.

The ride was very silent. Carolynn only stole a few glances but she kept quiet the entire time. Leaving Annette with her thoughts. She had never felt so discouraged until she really had to admit to herself that she really had nothing. She had to leave everything at the hotel this time, except her keys, wallet, phone (which were already in her pants), her laptop (which was already in her car) and the most important thing of all, her daughter. There really was no time. She began to recall all the years spent running. Every fight, every slap, every bruise, every painful; gut-wrenching moment. The farther away they got from the dinner, the more she thought. The more she thought, the more drained and sicker she felt. She couldn't see any of the landscaping. Thank goodness, she wasn't driving because after a few seconds the road in front of them all but disappeared. Leaving them to float in a cloud of black smog. Perfect for her mood.

"Now we are coming up on our turn off. You need to make sure you hold on tight. It could get bumpy, seeing as how I can barely see the potholes."

Moments, after they made the turn off the truck, dipped down and shot back up so fast that Annette nearly jumped out of her seat. She braced herself again, hearing her companion giggle in the seat next to her. A bit of humiliation flushed her cheeks but she had been warned. The road they were on seemed to go on forever. She wasn't sure if it really was twisting or just the woman next to her trying to miss more potholes. After about ten minutes she saw outlines of buildings come into view. The smog so thick she couldn't really make out any of them.

They stopped the truck in front of what Annette could make out as a white house. "We're here. Home sweet home. Now let's get you two inside and this little one into bed."

Cautiously Annette got out of the truck. The four other potholes they hit had taken a toll on her rump but she would never admit it. She unstrapped her daughter and proceeded to follow Carolynn inside.

****

"You worthless bitch." A low growl came from his throat just before he slapped her hard. Her head snapped back but she didn't fall since he had her hair wrapped around his other fist. "You never listen, you worthless bitch." Curling his free hand into a ball, he drew it back and punched her hard. She cried out in pain. Sparks glittering her eyes. Felt the pulsing after a few minutes. She didn't even realize he had dropped her to the ground. He was ready to kick her just as she heard a muffled cry followed by a cough. She knew he had heard it too. She saw him put his raised boot back down and turn his head in the direction of the noise. The closet! He had a half-crooked smile on his lips. That smile was so menacing it shook the very core of her. "You deserve everything you get slut." Her head began to get cloudy, her eye hurt bad, adjoined with searing pain grasping all over her. But as she saw him move closer to the closet she screamed.

At first, she didn't remember where she was. Shooting straight up with a large hand grasping her arm and shaking her she swung and connected with her assailant. She heard his low moan and backed into the corner of the bed. The bed! She looked around noticing the wooden furniture. The windows open just a bit with the breeze coming in. Her pulse began to slow a bit, her memory coming back in pieces as she started to fully wake up. Remembering that she fell asleep after she arrived at the dinner and not remembering anything until this morning. This morning! She heard a low grumble near the door. The man grasping his shoulder at the end of the bed made another moan as he worked on where she had hit him. She hit him!

"Oh, I am so sorry!" She began to scramble to the edge of the bed only to stop midway and back up again. "Who are you? What are you doing in here?" Her voice rising a notch.

Chapter 2

He damn well didn't need this, this morning. He knew he should have stayed out last night. The nice blonde waitress offered him a good time and a free meal when he woke up, but his grandma had told him she needed him to be home to help out. So here he was. He was definitely not expecting to wake up hearing a soul startling scream. Thinking the place was being robbed he got up and ran towards the noise. A McPherson was never once known to back down from a fight, or a woman in need.

When he had burst in he expected to see something a lot different then what he witnessed. The lady sat up with tears streaming down her face. He took in the features of her and only saw weary pain. But trying to wake her up had only caused him a bit more pain to his ego then he would have liked. Damn, she could hit. His shoulder was already getting sore.

While rubbing it again he looked over at her to see deep emerald color eyes staring back at him. Those were the most beautiful eyes he had ever seen. He felt something stir in his chest. Taking note that she was folding her arms over her chest he realized she was still waiting on an answer.

After tearing his eyes away to blindly stare at a spot behind her he replied. "Well, I came running after I heard a loud scream. Only I found the cause of it to be you." Rubbing his arm again, "And it seems I got a nice right hook for my troubles."

Looking at her again he saw a bit of sympathy in her eyes and something else. He almost thought he saw a hint of heat too. No, he had it wrong. Shaking off the notion he looked at her again. He noticed her eyes kept wandering lower and lower. Then a pretty blush crept up her neck as she looked back up at his face. He looked down to see what was so interesting only to find out he had crawled out of bed in nothing but his boxers.

"Oh. I'm…" Stopping only when he realized that all she had on was a form-fitting top. He could see through that shirt almost too well to not notice she had on a white cotton bra underneath. Daring to graze his eyes lower he saw her hunched back on her heels with only matching white cotton panties on to cover her bottom. Exposing her toned tanned legs. His hands were begging to run his fingers over them. When he felt something begin to stir in his boxers, he mentally shafted himself. "I'm sorry. I'll leave you to get dressed." He quickly spun around and left.

****

Annette was left feeling more embarrassed and confused than when she had first woken up. She still hadn't gotten his name. Not believing she had so openly assessed him. She felt her cheeks get hot again just remembering how hard and smooth his chest looked. Not a hair on him. His arms are so toned and tan. A working man's arms. Arms meant to hold you and keep you safe. Arms she wished could hold her and make her feel like she was safe again. She chided herself for even letting herself fantasize about that. It was useless to think in that direction. She told herself years ago she would never let a man get that close to her where she would rely on his false security again. Letting them get close meant they could hurt her. And she was not about to let any man hurt her ever again!

Ugh but those eyes. The color of steel. They got even darker when they looked at her. She remembered how he had taken his time to look at every inch of her. Making her feel quite exposed. It surprised her how she had actually enjoyed having his eyes on her, even for that brief moment. She even noticed the effect it had begun to take on him. That alone had made her start to feel warm inside.

Her thoughts were brought back to the present when there was a slight rap on the door. Startled she pulled the covers up to cover herself. "Yes?"

"Deary, may I come in?" Letting out a breath of air she told Carolynn to enter. She pushed opened the door and placed the few items she was carrying on the dresser. "I brought you a few towels and some clean clothes. Now they may be a bit big Dear but they will do for now. Just leave your dirty clothes on the floor. I'll see they get washed." She went to leave, but stopped and turned around. "Oh and Miss Holly is downstairs eating her pancakes. That little dear sure can eat." And with a smile on her lips she left, closing the door behind her.

The thoughtfulness and compassion brought tears to her eyes. She needed to stop crying or she was going to turn soft and that was not an option for her. She had to remain tough, ready to move at any given time. Speaking of any given time, she needed to get her car and get moving. Annette crawled out of bed to take a shower. She picked up the clothes left for her and walked into the nicest bathroom she has ever been in. Sparkling granite countertop with giant hanging mirror. A toilet closet in one corner and against the wall a shower that had so many jets, she was a bit confused on which to turn on. After trying a few, she finally figured out how to handle the knobs and turned the water as hot as she could stand it. The heat relaxing her skin and reviving her spirit the tiniest bit.

In less than five minutes she was dressed and following voices downstairs leading her to the kitchen. She leaned up against the door jamb when she realized no one had heard her. The man from earlier sitting with his back to her, talking to a familiar voice. She couldn't see her daughter but she heard her all the same. They were cutting up what was left of her pancakes and counting the pieces.

Not being noticed gave her time to leisurely look him over again. He had a strong firm back, leading down to a well-toned bottom. His hair was the color of a chestnut. So rich but cut low just below his ears. A door opened behind her and as he turned his head in that direction a lock of hair fell to the curve just below his eye. She couldn't help but think how adorable he must have been as a boy. Their eyes met and a wicked smile came to his lips. Sensing he was remembering what happened earlier brought another blush to her cheeks. She couldn't believe the effect he was having on her. Making her act like a school girl again and she didn't like it one bit.

"Well now. Look who joined us for breakfast. "Gliding past her Carolynn laid down a basket full of flowers over on the counter and turned back around. "Now Austin, where are your manners?! We have a guest in this house." Taking up the clucking noise again that is starting to become oddly comforting in its own way. He jumped up and offered her his chair while asking if she would like something to drink.

As soon as her daughter realized she was there she jumped up and ran to her. Hugging tightly to her leg and rambling on, Annette only able to catch every other word. "Mama… I ate like a big girl… Mr. 'Stin he's nice…"

"Alright honey, alright. Calm down, baby." Leaning down to hug her and kiss her cheek. "Have you went potty yet?"

Nodding her head, "Yes I did! I don't have to go yet." She looked at the floor. That was Annette's queue that her daughter was just being a bit stubborn and didn't want to go again.

"Honey you need to try and go again. We have to leave soon and get the car. I'd like for you to at least try okay?" Lifting her chin and crouching so her daughter would look into her face. "Please?"

"Okay, Mommy." Standing to follow her daughter into the bathroom only for her daughter to push her back. "No, I want to do it! I can do it."

"Okay, okay. If you have a problem yell." She watched with a little bit of pride as her daughter walked into the bathroom and closed the door.

"She's a bright young gal." Turning to find Austin standing close behind her. So close she could smell him. A hint of cologne mixed with the mustiness of sweat and hay. A man of the earth. It was like honey to her senses. She closed her eyes when she breathed in.

"Is everything okay ma'am?" Oh, how that deep voice moved her. The southern drawl adding to the effect, giving her goosebumps. *Stop it, Stop it!*

Chapter 3

Austin caught his breath when she opened her eyes. Her eyes were so dark. The same desire from earlier clearly written all over them. There was no questioning it this time. She bit her lower lip and then grazed her tongue across the surface. Making him want to press his mouth to hers. He wondered if they were as soft as he imagined. He also noticed the glaze that swept over those intriguing eyes the next instant. That's when he saw the black eye. How could he have missed it before? He could tell something was going on inside her head and wished he knew what it was.

She rubbed her arms and looked away from him at something that was more interesting on the floor. That's when he took in her attire. Nice fitting jeans curved to her legs and he would bet they form-fitted to her butt perfectly. A pair that had been left from when his mother was alive. The shirt was one of his old ones from when he was younger. A bit baggy around the sleeves but she had taken and twisted the back of the flannel shirt up so that it clung to her body. Molding to the full breast beneath. He caught a glimpse of the top of one of her full mounds through the open buttons at the top and inwardly groaned.

He needed to stop torturing himself. First chance he gets he is finding an intimate distraction. He needed it. It has been too long. Realizing he was staring again he looked away, but not before she noticed. He felt himself grow hot around the ears and knew she'd see it.

"Is there something wrong?" She sounded small but not defenseless. Hearing the underlying bite to her words.

"Well, I was just admiring the shirt. I think I wore it about fifteen years ago." He couldn't believe he had said that. He was anticipating a slap or something. Instead, she seemed to get more self-conscious. Hugging herself a bit tighter. He ran his fingers through his hair. *Doesn't she know how amazing she looks?*

"Look I only meant it looks a lot better on you than it ever did on me." Wow! Where was this coming from? He was never this forward. Although it seemed to relax her a bit after understanding that he was complimenting her. His reward was a stunning smile that shows her perfect teeth. The smile went as quickly as it had come when they were greeted again by a little tyke in a red shirt and jean trousers.

"Sorry, but she needed to be changed. She made a bit of a mess in the sink. Hope you don't mind?" Carolynn looked almost cheerful about the situation. Apparently, neither of them noticed her go into the bathroom just down the hall. Too distracted by each other.

"It's okay. She has done worse before." Bending down to whisper in her daughter's ear. "Honey we have to get ready to go. Are you done eating?"

Her daughter just nodded her head but without any smile. She felt an ache in her chest when she looked at her. She wished she could just let her be a child, if only for a little while. To be able to stay somewhere that she knew people and could play. But such things were not reasonable for them right now and wasting idle time was not an option.

"Well, Austin can drive you to your car. I need him to pick up some things in town anyway."

Carolynn scurried away with Holly trailing behind to grab her list, leaving them alone.

****

He ran his fingers through his hair several times giving off a sense of uneasiness. She could relate. Especially after the things he had said to her. She still wasn't sure if he was complimenting her or flirting with her. She couldn't help but admit she was intrigued and a bit interested, but she wouldn't own to any more than that. There isn't any room for fantasies in her thoughts. A piece of his hair fell over to touch his cheek. *Dang, he is hot.*

He was the first to break the silence. "So, Gran told me you left your car at Mickey's? You just come into town last night?" She looked up to find those wonderfully bright eyes staring at her once again.

"Yea. I'm just passing through; Carolynn was nice enough to offer me a place to sleep. Well more like tied my hands behind my back, but it was still nice of her." They both chuckled.

He went to speak again but the crash of dishes turned both their attentions to the sink behind him. They saw Holly dropping the plates from breakfast into the sink. Since she was so short, she had to stand on her tiptoes and jump a bit. Still not quite being able to see over the top of the sink. Smiling at her daughter she went to move to help her but Austin was faster. He was next to her not only helping her but picking her up and letting her do it herself. It was the most perfect picture she could imagine as man and child worked together. Making her long for better times.

Holly pulled some of the suds out of the sink and wiped them all over his face. Annette put her

hand up to cover her mouth from laughing out loud.
She almost expected him to get mad, but then when
Holly giggled, he laughed. Long and loud. A deep full
joyous laugh. It curled around her and warmed her
from inside.

"Well don't you two look so adorable together.
Like a bunch of silly soap heads." The giggle that
Carolynn let out made her sound ten years younger.
Pulling back her eyes, making little crow's feet at the
corners more defined. "I miss the sounds of the little
ones." A more sentimental tone to her voice.

Austin began cleaning off the suds on himself
and Holly. Sitting her back down on the floor. "Mr.
'Stin, I wanna again! Again!" Holly jumping up and
down trying to get him to pick her back up.

"We need to get cleaned up kiddo. Your mama
needs to get moving." He smiled bigger to show he
wasn't trying to scold her. "You want to go for a walk
while your mom gets ready?" He touched the end of
her nose. These small moments touched her in ways
she couldn't even explain. She wished she could give
her daughter a father who played with her.

Lost in her own thoughts she didn't notice they
had left the room till she heard the screen door closing
behind them. The familiar clucking coming from over
her shoulder. She turned to see Carolynn smiling at
her like she had an answer to a secret. "What?"
Saying it a little harsher than she meant to.

"Nothing Dearie. I brought your clean clothes,
and here is the list I need. Can you give it to him for
me? These old knees are aching. I think I'm gonna
head up and take a nap." Carolynn leaned in for a hug
and squeezed her tighter than she was expecting.
"You take care now you hear me? Keep that little dear

safe." Only after Annette nodded her agreeance did the other lady kiss her cheek and leave.

Watching her walk away she felt like there was more Carolynn wanted to say. The familiar ache of wanting a family almost overwhelmed her for a second. She wanted to belong somewhere, so much sometimes that she thought she would die from it. In the back of her mind though she knew it was not an option for them right now, so she just brushed it off and walked outside.

Chapter 4

Standing here against the fence with Holly on his shoulders clapping her hands, while watching the horses made him wish for a family. He began to wonder why he hadn't felt this need sooner. He was getting older and settling down he decided, was becoming more appealing to him. Wanting to hear the sounds of kids running around the yard seemed surreal to him. He could remember him and his brothers always roughing around out here. He used to find peace and security within these lands, and that is exactly what he would want to give his own kids.

He had just bent down to let Holly off his back when *she* walked onto the porch. Those jeans hugging her just right as the sun shone down on her hair. Making it sparkle and light up. Gorgeous shades of gold and brown trailing down her shoulders. He unconsciously flexed his chest muscles.

Holly had run past him and up the steps to be picked up by her mom. The two of them so happy to be near one another. She kissed her head as she put her back down. Holly jumping up and down saying something about the horses before she took off to stand next to the fence and point.

Everything moved as if in slow motion. Watching as this beautiful woman came walking towards him, looking at him under long lashes that were lowered from the glaring sun. Having to look down into her face he couldn't help but see the trickle of sweat that rolled down her neck to disappear between the crease of two perfect peaks. He wanted to follow that trail with his tongue.

Coughing to keep the focus off of the growing erection in his pants he turned slightly so that he could focus on something else to calm his nerves. He decided to watch the mare out in the pasture eating instead. After a few seconds, his body relaxed enough for him to turn back around.

"We didn't get off on the right foot this morning. I'm afraid I still don't know your name?" Noticing the look of a question in her eyes and the slight flicker of something across those eyes. Was that dear he saw? It was there one second and gone so fast, he wasn't sure if that was what he saw.

"My name is Annette. And you already met Holly, my daughter." He stuck out his hand and shook hers before saying, "The names Austin." She smiled at him and he felt a burst of warmth in his chest. He wanted to stay right there all day but she pulled her hand away to hand him a piece of paper. Leaving his palm cold where hers had been.

"Your Gran wanted you to have this." He took the small piece of paper and reviewed the list. Sighing he stuffed it in his shirt pocket.

"Are you ready to go?"

"Of course. Come on Holly!" Was it just him or did she just get very distant and rigid next to him? Almost like she was pulling away. He tried to ignore it and helped them into the truck.

The way into town was filled with the adorable little tyke between them rambling on about horses. Talking about each one she saw. Austin was only able to get in a word here or there because of her excitement. He grasped that she didn't get out much, or around animals for that matter. He found out that they spent a lot of their time in the car.

"So, what do you do when you're home?"

Lowering her eyes to her feet, and mumbling so softly he almost couldn't hear it, "We don't have one."

"Honey, don't bother Mr. Austin. He's driving." Annette patted her daughter's leg in reassurance.

"It is no trouble. She can talk as much as she would like." He gave a grin as Holly looked up at him. She smiled but he could see the glimmer of tears in her big round eyes. The same green as her mothers, but with a hint of blue in them. Knowing the conversation was over he put his focus back on the road.

Thinking about that sweet girl's answer made him ache for her. How can they not have a home? Was Annette just not a reliable woman, forcing them to move around? Or, was there something else at play? Was she running from something, or towards something? So many questions. He couldn't imagine what it felt like not to have somewhere you could feel like you belonged. The ranch was his safe haven in times of need.

He saw the flashing lights in the distance. The police cars coming more into view the closer he got to Mickey's. They pulled into the parking lot and parked right next to a police cruiser, just as Sam came rushing out of the dinner. Sam was already talking when he started to roll down the window. "—They are still looking for whoever it is. They need to talk to you now. This has never happened here before and it is unnerving some of the locals." Stopping to catch her breath.

"Whoa, slow down. Now, what happened? Who needs to ask questions?"

"Sorry. I'm just a bit flustered. Mickey got a call this mornin' from the sheriff. A passerby saw someone busting up a car." Giving a sympathetic look to Annette, "They want to talk to you dear. Turns out it was your car they were trashin. They called Carolynn after I told them she had taken you home last night but she said you were already on your way here. Nothing like this has ever happened here, so you can imagine how people are taking it."

Anger coursed through him. Who the heck could have done something like this and in his hometown. One looks over at Annette and he got even more enraged. The woman he had talked to just moments earlier seemed to have faded. She was huddled up in her seat against the window. Her legs pulled up against her chest and looking like she was about to cry. Something primal raged inside of him.

"Alright, Sam. We'll be right over." Sam looked from one to the other and nodded in retreat. He rolled the window back up and blew out a breath. Holly had gotten really quiet beside him. That only made his protective instincts kick in. He wanted so badly to grab both of them and pull them into his lap, to tell them everything would be alright. He knew he couldn't do that, so instead, he rubbed Holly's head, giving her the biggest smile, he could muster when she looked at him. Her own small smile rewarding him in return when she looked at him before turning to look at her mother. He tried placing a hand on her arm, but Annette jumped at his touch and seemed to huddle into herself even more.

Frowning he unbuckled himself and got out of the truck. Walked around to her door and prying it open he unbuckled her too. "What are you doing?" Without answering he turned her in her seat and wrapped his arms around her. At first, she stiffened at his touch, but then she began to relax. She slid her arms under his and around his back. Clinging to him. She buried her face in his shoulder, but he could tell she was trying to not cry. She felt so good in his arms. Smelling of honeysuckle and all woman. He only wished he could take some of the burdens off her. If only for a few minutes. He noticed the sheriff walking towards them, so he put up a finger indicating to give them a minute. The sheriff nodded in agreement and went back over towards the other vehicle where the other officers were.

****

Feeling so weak and only wanting to give up, knowing she couldn't, she clung to the only person holding it together. Literally. She had begun to have an anxiety attack and she knew the cause. Austin had come to her, without her telling him to, and comforted her. She knew she should push him back and tell him she could handle it. But she didn't want to. He felt so good and he was actually relaxing her some. Everything about him was making her relax. He warmth. The way he smelled like spice and sweat. The feel of his skin against her cheek and arms. The way he held on so tight, she never wanted him to let her go. She missed all those things the moment he pulled back and held onto her upper arms. Looking into her eyes, "Are you ok to go talk to them?". She turned and looked at her baby girl, who was staring at her hands in silence. Dropping his hands to his knees as she turned to her in the seat and unbuckled her to pull her to her lap. Her daughter's arms wrapping around her neck and nuzzling her cheek to her chest. Remembering why she had to stay strong gave her courage.

Annette turned to Austin, never letting go of her daughter. "Let's get this over with." He helped her down from the truck and she blew out a breath, straightened herself as best she could with a toddler in her arms, and walked over to the crime scene.

The next two hours were hard. The sedan had been torn apart and smashed in. Broken glass littering the ground around the vehicle, rips in the seats like claws, mats were thrown out of the car, and all of this along with a dismantled steering column. The police had mentioned it must have been the work of a lunatic. Boy, they had no idea. The sheriff and his deputies, along with some of the police from the neighboring towns had questioned all three of them. She held her breath as they asked her daughter simple questions that soon lead to more expansive ones. Leaving her no choice but to go into detail about her past relationship. She hated that her daughter had to relive the experiences repeatedly. She had been through enough. Seeing Austin's face go from concern to disgust, and then to heated rage after going over all the facts just made it that much worse. The police pulled her aside to speak in more detail about specific facts over the last few encounters made her even more embarrassed.

Her daughter was getting so tired she was yawning every few seconds. Austin walked over to her and picked her up. "I'll go tuck her in, in the truck for a nap." She wanted to protest but he was right. She needed sleep and she was probably going to be a while still. Seeing him walk away with her daughter gave her a feeling like this is where she was meant to be. With this man. Mentally shaking herself, she turned back to the sheriff. After an hour of conversation with the sheriff and other police officers, they told her not to go anywhere while they talked amongst themselves. Leaving her alone with her thoughts.

She told herself that when they were alone, she would explain. These people deserved an explanation as to why their lives might be in upheaval over her. She also found that she wanted to tell Austin about everything and that shocked her the most. She had never wanted to spill everything to anyone. The only person who knows the whole story was her best friend and publisher Roxanne.

Roxanne! How could she have forgotten to call her! She must have been so worried by now. Annette always made it a point to call her at least once a day to check-in. She still had to send in the synopsis of her new manuscript. Suddenly remembering her laptop was still in the car, or at least hoping it was, ran for her car. Startling the police officers and drawing the attention of Austin. She vaguely noticed the police officers running after her, shouting something. With the doors already open on the sedan, she bent over and searched the hem of the passenger seat. She had sewn this spot in the first time he had found her. Once she had found the familiar zipper, she tugged on it and the familiar zip filled her pounding eardrums.

Reaching inside she let out a loud rush of air she had been holding. It was there! Along with her journal, some personal photos, a wallet with extra cash, and her extra cellphone for emergencies. She couldn't believe it. Tears stung at her eyes as relief flooded her. She stood up with the computer bag full of items clinging to her chest. Everyone had stood still and stared at her. Austin looked at her with puzzlement and concern. The officer who had been rushing after her and shouting had taken the items and inspected them. When she explained the hidden compartment and that those items were for work, and personal means he gave them back to her. Slinging the strap over her head and around her shoulder felt so comforting. If only for a moment.

The sheriff, whom Annette finally paid attention long enough to remember his name was Sheriff Townsend but he asked to be called Tony. He was going to have them both stay in the county jail for the night. He said this was to make sure they both stayed safe until he could find another accommodation for them to have protection. All Annette wanted to do was leave. Pack all her meager belongings, get her daughter and keep moving. But with it getting later in the day, and having no vehicle, she had realized getting out of this town was going to be harder said than done. Austin, who had been listening to their conversation, chimed in.

"I can have them stay at the ranch, Tony. It would be better than sitting in a cell all night." Tony looked from her to Austin. Rubbing the bridge of his nose in consideration or annoyance, or maybe both. "Whoever did this might come back and I surely doubt this was just a warning."

"They will be safe at the house. Besides, you do not want a little girl to wake up in a cell. She is already upset and frightened. I doubt even you want that." Austin standing so close to her now, his arm pressing up against hers.

Tony let out a breath of air in defeat. "Alright. Only for the time being. I will be by the ranch in the morning to go over more details and to check-in. Ms. O'Leary – ", He said giving her a hard stare, "Do not go leaving town. Not only for your safety but that of your daughters. Someone did this and although we believe we know who, it could be anyone. Until we get the report back on the fingerprint analysis we cannot be sure." He then turned and walked away. Leaving them there, with more worry than reassurance.

Her feet felt like they were in quicksand walking back to the truck. So many thoughts running through her mind. The adrenaline rushes her body had felt was cooling down and now came the tired feeling that always followed.

The sun started to make orange hues across the sky as it began its descent. A light breeze that swept through the window of the truck was cooling off her skin. There was something rhythmic about the sounds of her daughter napping, the wind brushing against her cheek, and watching the land as it passed by. The calmness of the moment mixed with the drained feeling had her resting her head on her arm on the window sill.

It wasn't till after seven when Austin finally finished getting his list of supplies and they finally started their trek back to the ranch. By then she had already taken a power nap and her little munchkin had woken up to make her own conversation in the backseat. The whole ride home she was internally anxious. She wanted to explain some to him, to try and make him understand, but not knowing what his reaction would have set her on edge a bit. She didn't know when it happened but somehow, she started to care about what he thought, and that bothered her in more ways than one.

Every time she felt she was going to start a conversation she would look over at him, and then stop herself. A feeling of shame and embarrassment would hold her back. So, after a few attempts, she just gave up altogether and stared straight ahead.

They pulled to a stop in front of the farmhouse just as the sun was leaving the sky. Casting darkness over the land and buildings. Austin had been quiet the whole time, no doubt lost in his own thoughts. Annette didn't want to disturb him or annoy him anymore then she assumed he was. It was a bad situation she had put them all in and she only hoped that he wouldn't regret his decision about letting them stay. She told herself she would rather run again then put her daughter in a jail cell till they found him. He startled her out of her thoughts when he spoke. "I'm going to take her to bed." He got out of the truck, unbuckled and picked up a sleeping Holly. She got out of the truck and watched him walk towards the house, "I'll be back down to talk to you." And he was gone.

Chapter 5

Carrying that little girl in the house felt so surreal. He held a little piece of life in his hands and he wanted to protect her. He wanted to protect them both. That meant he was getting attached and that was dangerous. He barely knew them, heck what he knew of them could fit into the church collection basket. His arm was getting a little bit wet from the drool starting to pool out of her little mouth but he didn't mind. He loved the weight filling his arms and the tiny coos she made. Gran was up in the Livingroom when he walked towards the stairs. Holding up a finger to stop her from getting up out of the armchair. He turned and walked Holly upstairs to bed. After making sure she was tucked in and the corner lamp was on because kids needed night lights right – he silently walked out of the room. Making sure her door was creaked open before he made his way back downstairs.

He could not get over the feeling that even though something serious was going on with Annette, they were right where they were meant to be. He already decided tomorrow he was going to try and talk to her about all of this. Tonight, he has a feeling she may be overwhelmed and need to cool down. Or maybe he just needed time to take it all in. A lot happened with the 24 hours he has known her.

Gran was sitting up knitting in her favorite chair when he got back downstairs. "Austin, come in here. I want to know what happened at the diner."

Hanging in the doorway he casually said, "I will explain everything in the morning, Gran. I don't even really know myself yet. Can we call it a night and I will fill you in when everyone has had a good night's rest?"

He knew she wanted answers but he really had none right then and there. The whole incident at Mickey's wasn't even clear to him yet. He wanted answers himself still but he needed time to get them. There was no way Annette was going to just blurt it all out. Not from the way she closed in on herself earlier. Time is what they both needed. Something which he was fully aware of but it was not always able to be given.

He rubbed his hand over his chin before moving on to the front door. He heard his Gran call out that she was going to bed just as the screen door shut closed behind him. He stood there in the breeze letting his eyes adjust to the cool Montana night sky.

****

That was it? He left her standing next to the truck alone. All her insecurities hit her all at once. Felt pulled down by them. What if he was angry at her for not telling him sooner? What if he wanted her gone in the morning? What if he was mad at her for getting them involved? What would she do if the horror from a few days ago found her here? She could not stand hurting these people she had begun to care about and that only meant one thing to her. She couldn't stay.

After walking over to the fence, she leaned against it. The creaking sounds from her weight showing its age. The few horses in the pen didn't even give her a second thought. They just kept munching on their grass as if nothing else in the world mattered. Although for them, it was the truth. What would she do if he showed up here and begun where he left off?

Instead this time he wouldn't just be hurting her. There would be bystanders and that could mean he would become more dangerous. Grief and regret filled her up inside. So much so, that she began to feel a bit nauseated with it. Crossing her arms on the fence and bowing her head just as the tears began rolling down her cheeks.

She heard the screen door closing. She could hear him approach before he spoke. Listening to his boots hitting the dirt patches. When he finally did speak, he sounded exhausted. Just as completely used up from the emotional toll of the day as she felt. "OK. I don't want to go around in circles. I do not want to hear facts from other people. I want to only hear them from you. So, can you please, tell me what all happened and what is going on."

When she didn't answer him at first, he softly spoke her name. The soft plea of her name was so soothing that it made more tears fall. She stared at the dust her tears were kicking up as they fell. He moved in front of her and slowly urged her chin up with his palm. She noticed behind him that a full silvery moon had risen in the sky. So bright it cast a soft glow on the earth around them.

She knew he was going to speak. He had parted his lips to say something. However, when he saw her red-rimmed eyes and felt her wet cheeks with the back of his hand, she saw something change in the features of his face. He caressed her jaw and cheek with his thumb and her eyes fluttered closed. The sensation of someone else comforting her, like this, made her heart skip a beat. He was so close to her that he could feel the warmth radiating off his chest through his shirt. She took in a deep breath, and her nostrils were filled with that familiar scent of him. *Almighty, he smelled so good!*

Just as she began to wonder what his lips would taste like, he kissed her. So many emotions rammed into her at once. Surrender, fear, embarrassment, and so many others. Her first instinct was to pull away. She knew it was wrong and that she shouldn't be doing this. She needed to talk to him. He had asked her to. But his lips were so tender; his kiss so delicate that she found herself leaning into him. By pure reflex, she wrapped her arms around his neck. He wrapped his other arm, that was not holding onto her face, around her back. The closer he pulled her to him, the more passionate his kisses got.

The last shred of consciousness fled her as his tongue found hers. He produced a groan from deep in his throat, so primal it sent goosebumps sprinkling her skin. He hauled her against him, eliminating any empty space between them. His prominent arousal pressing ever so urgently against her stomach. Suddenly her clothes felt like an unwanted barrier between them. She wanted them off. Now!

Tearing her mouth away to catch her breath, "You want to go inside?"

She could see the lift at the corner of his mouth. Making his rugged boyish features more handsome with the glow of the moon upon his skin. "At this moment, there is nothing I want more than you in my bed." His voice husky and laced with excitement. He lifted her up and carried her up the porch steps. Placing his finger to his mouth, "Shhhhh. We have to be quiet. Gran just went to bed." Another one of his smiles pulled at something in her chest. She felt like they were in high school and could get caught at any moment. He opened the screen door with his foot and began climbing the stairs with her in his arms. Their much-needed conversation forgotten at the moment.

Once inside he placed her down on her feet and kissed her again. This time a bit more tender and relaxed, rather than the fever of the first kiss. Annette putting her hand under his shirt, splaying her fingers over the hard-taunt muscles beneath. She made a low sigh. He was everything she wanted and more. If she did this now how was she ever going to let go? He tugged at the hem of her shirt, trying to get her to lift her arms. A flicker of fear went through her. She didn't want him to witness her bruises. Being beaten pretty badly this last time left her with some dark ones she couldn't hide. Although, he did not mention anything about her eye earlier. In the mirror, this morning she noticed it began to start changing color around the edges. It was noticeable.

"We can take it slow if you're unsure. Or we can stop now." Still holding her against him, he pulled his head back far enough to look down into her eyes. "But I need to know one way or the other before we take this any further."

"No. No, I'm- I'm fine. Just anxious. It's been a while for me." *Well, at least it's partly true.* It has been a long time for her. At least with another man that wasn't forcing her to do something. She hasn't had much time to get involved with anyone, let alone think about sex these past few years.

He gave another one of his little sexy smiles, "I can take care of that." In one swift motion, he had her shirt and bra off. Her clothes hadn't even hit the floor before he began trailing kisses down her neck and between her breasts. Becoming increasingly self-conscious about the bruises that have to be visible in the dim moonlight of the room. She was going to pull his head back up, that is until he took a nipple into this mouth. Sucking in her breath at contact and instinctively arching into him. All conscious thoughts escaping her once again. He took his time leisurely. Suckling one nipple and then the other, until he was fully satisfied.

Not being able to wait any longer, she pulled him back up to her mouth. She had to touch him. Had to feel all of him. Deepening her kiss was her way of showing him her urgency. When he grabbed her butt to rub her against his erection, she got more excited. *Oh my! He was so thick with his pants on!* She knew then that it would not take him long to finish. He pulled off his shirt and exposing himself to her. The motion of it made her breath catch in her throat. Annette knew she needed to feel him. She began trailing languid kisses from his mouth, down his shoulders, and over his bare chest.

Slowly, at least what she hoped was slow and did not seem too eager, she got down on her knees. Kissing her way down his chest as she went. Stopping when her lips found the top of his jeans. Kneeling down in front of him she watched him. She wanted to see his reaction to her cupping him and stroking him through his jeans. Excitement pooling between her legs as he closed his eyes and tilted his head back toward the ceiling. A moan escaping his mouth as he laced his fingers through her hair.

He released her hair as she began unbuttoning his jeans. Annette took her time undoing his pants and pushing them down over his hips. She marveled at how perfect he was after she freed him. He was not only strong and handsome but very well endowed too. Stroking him for a few seconds showed to push him towards the edge. Not wanting him to go to early, she stopped herself. A soft whine escaped his lips. He said her name so softly she almost didn't hear him. Their eyes locked and suddenly she understood he needed this just as much as she did. She watched his eyes roll back and she felt his hands grab the back of her head, as she took him into her mouth.

Sensing he was almost there and becoming increasingly excited herself, she took him deeper into her mouth. Moving faster and faster. He growled, predatorily, deep down in this chest. She tried to slow down; Pull him back some from the edge, but he would have none of it. Before she knew it, he grabbed the back of her head. Holding her there he thrust himself all the way into her mouth and exploded. The taste of him filling her senses.

After regaining some of his composure from the weak feeling in his legs, he slowly released his hold on her hair. "Damn. That was... just... damn. You are so sexy." He pulled her up to meet claim a kiss. "Sorry it was so sudden. It's been a while for me too and I just couldn't hold it any longer."

"It's alright." His hands fondling her bottom.

He picked her up, "No. Now it's your turn.", he said as he laid her down on the bed. After making her nipples into aching peaks again with his tongue, he undid her pants. Slowly he moved lower. Licking and biting as he went. When he grazed the bruises on her hips she winced.

"Sorry. I didn't mean to bite too hard." She didn't say anything. She just let him believe that was the problem. He continued his path, only this time a lot softer with his nibbling. Lingering on her inner thigh after getting her pants down around her ankles. He left her pants that way as he lifted her legs and moved in between them. Placing her legs over his shoulders.

****

He knew she was close to release even before he touched her. The moment he grazed his finger over her swollen center she moaned and arched her back. He couldn't stand it. The beauty of her beneath him. Her sensual yet powerful pull over him. "Tell me what you want", as he stared at all of her open before him.

He saw her bite her lip. Was she excited or nervous? While waiting for an answer he stroked his fingers in and out of her. Noticing how increasingly wet she was becoming with every movement. That whimper of a need to release sent chills down his back. *God, she was so sexy!* After what seemed like hours but was only a few seconds he heard his name from her lips. "Austin", she repeated.

"Yes baby, tell me what you want."

"I want you to taste me." Unaware that her plea would affect him so deeply, he drove his fingers into her. He growled again as a loud noise escaped her lips. His growl both startling her and thrilling her. Wasting no time with her omission, he withdrew his fingers and took her wholly into his mouth. Suckling and prodding his tongue into her sweet center. She let out a cry and thrashed her head back and forth. She tried to open her legs wider but her bound ankles would only allow for her to go so far. Forcing her to deal with the sensational torment he was unleashing.

He pulled out of her and suckled on her hot little nub. Using only his lips and tongue. Bringing her closer and closer as he applied more pressure. Not being able to take it any longer she let go. Completely exploded in waves, crying out his name into the darkness. It was the most beautiful thing he had ever heard.

Austin laid down on the bed, cradling her next to him. She laid her head on his chest, "I love the sound of your heartbeat."

"Mmmmm." Was all that came from him before he kissed her head and both fell into a deep sleep.

Chapter 6

She awoke to the sun shining in her eyes. For a brief moment, she thought she may have dreamed last night but her body was telling her otherwise. Muscles ached in places she didn't even remember she had. A smile spreading across her face as she replayed last night in her head. They had satisfied each other, yes, but she had felt something more. When she laid in his arms, it was like a piece of her was restored somehow. She wanted to stay in bed for as long as possible. She wasn't ready to give up this feeling just yet, but her reality wasn't about happily ever after's.

She could remember him redressing her very slowly. Taking his time to thoroughly kiss her. When she was fully clothed, he picked her up and took her to her bed. Leaving her there to sleep alone. She could feel something was bothering him, Lord knew she had her own demons to deal with, but he kept all his thoughts all to himself. Something she could relate to but didn't make her feel any better.

She sat up just as her daughter burst into the room. "Mommy! Mommy!" She ran and jumped onto the bed. Bouncing up and down before Anette took it upon herself to start a tickling war. After both of them caught their breath, "Now baby, are you going to tell mommy why you are in her bed?"

Resuming her bouncing on the bed, "Mr. 'Stin said I to bring you down. They bo'fth want you." Annette could think of only one thing they would want to talk about and it sent a chill down her spine. No, she would do this. They all deserved an explanation. "Ok honey. Tell them I'll be right down."

Holly jumped off the bed and ran out of the room. Sighing she got out of bed, her reminiscing over with. She got a quick shower in the adjoining bathroom before she went downstairs to deal with the inevitable.

They were all sitting around the kitchen island when she made it downstairs. The chatter stopping as she entered the room. Sending out an eerie feeling about the room even though there was an open window basking everyone in sunlight. Hoping to find some warmth from Austin after what passed between them last night, but now all she felt was distance.

"Good Morning Deary. Can I get you something to drink?" Without waiting for an answer Carolynn walked away to pour a cup of tea and placed it on the counter in front of Annette. Annette took this as her cue to take a seat. Holly was grabbing biscuits off a plate from Carolynn.

"Honey- "Carolynn bent down, "Why don't you go into the Livingroom and watch cartoons for a bit. The grownups need to talk for a few moments." Annette pushed a lock of hair behind her daughter's ear.

"I love you munchkin." Giving butterfly kisses and squeezing her tight. Holly wiggling out of her arms to go run into the Livingroom. A few seconds and she hear the faint noise of the TV. Annette moved her focus to the individuals still in the kitchen. The silence felt like a wet blanket covering her. The anxiety of their discussion settling heavy in her chest. As she spoke she kept her gaze locked on the countertop and her hands folded in front of her.

"I don't know where to start. You will never know how sorry I am for putting you in the middle of this. It should have never happened and I will understand if you don't want me to stay here." Tears burned at the back of her eyes. She placed her hands over the back of her neck rubbing at the tension she felt.

"Now, now dear. We don't want you to leave." The clucking sound that followed soothe her for some reason.

She felt his stare before she heard him speak. He had remained silent until now and she thought it was because he was upset about what happened. "Tony, the sheriff called this mooring. He told me that he suspects it was your ex-husband that did this. Now tell me from your mouth what the hell is going on so we can figure out what we're gonna do."

Her head snapped up, all her tension was forgotten. Surely, she misheard something. His words didn't sound angry at all. In fact, they sounded very tender and what she saw in his eyes proved it. She saw compassion and understanding in him. She had never expected that. The unshed tears began to well in her eyes and she had to blink to keep them at bay. *I will not cry!*

She blew out a deep breath. Calming her nerves enough to try to explain everything. "Yes, he is my ex-husband. His name is Terry. Terry Handsbro. He was nice when I first met him. At first, I thought his slight control issue was because he knew what he wanted out of life and the drive to make everything perfect was what attracted me to him. I was very naive in those days." She took a sip from her tea to collect her thoughts before continuing.

"So how long were you two married?" Not sure if she senses just concern in his voice or if there was a bit of jealously within the subtext.

Lowering her eyes again she went on. "We said our vows five years ago this past August." I knew something wasn't right after our reception. He had punched the DJ in the face for just looking at me. But his protective issues got even worse as time went on. I wasn't allowed to have friends. My family wasn't allowed to visit me because he said they made a bad influence on me. I was going to leave once after the first time he hit me because he had fractured a rib, but the woman at the hospital had told us that I was 2 months pregnant. He was in the room with me you see."

"After hearing that he wouldn't leave my side for a minute. Always apologizing and trying to make it up to me. He became *too* nice. Letting me do things, within a limit. He would never let me out of his sight long enough to even use the bathroom at times." *Is this what it feels like to cave? To just give in?* Letting go of all her welled up emotions; being able to tell someone about this was like being reborn to her. All this stressful weight had been too much to bear all on her own.

Her shoulders slumping forward, "I know I may not have been the perfect woman. I caused problems, sometimes just because I wanted a fight. I needed a reason to cause the pain he was inflicting. That way it was a bit more bearable than just knowing he was doing it because he hated me for no reason. The rages became increasingly more violent after I had Holly." Some of the tears she was holding back leaked through her vision. She knew her cheeks were getting red from the embarrassing omission of her past, but she had to continue. "I tried not to scream so Holly couldn't hear it. I didn't need her tarnished by it either, but that only made the beatings worse. He wanted me to yell, he would even get excited by it." She heard Austin grab the glass on the counter and the screeching of the chair legs as he got up. Saw his feet as they moved to the sink. Annette lifted her eyes to see him standing with his back to her. His form so ridged it scared her.

She jumped at the sound of the glass breaking. At first, she thought he may have thrown it or even dropped it too hard, but as he turned around, she saw the blood trickling from his hand. He had crushed it with his bare hand. Letting out a little cry, Carolynn rushed to him and wrapped it with a towel. Annette was too much in shock to say anything. She only sat there and stared. That kind of rage scared the living daylights out of her because she knew what that kind of strength and unbridled anger could do. She had felt it.

"We need to get you to a doctor! Come on lets-"

"No." Austin didn't even look at Carolynn, who looked surprised. He had silenced her with one word as he locked his sights on her. She saw anger mixed with pain in those steel-colored eyes of his. Pain for her? She wasn't sure. "No. Please keep going. I need to hear this." He stayed leaning up against the sink with the towel wrapped hand. Carolynn began her clucking again as she took her seat.

"After Holly turned one, I knew I had to leave. After he had forced himself on me once again, he beat me savagely. I was sure he was going to kill me that time and I would have gladly let him end it all at that point if it wasn't for Holly. He had it in his mind that I had cheated on him. That Holly was a bastard child and that he was going to teach me a lesson." Adding air quotes for effect. "It took me days to recover from that one." She cradled her stomach at the memory. It made her so nauseated she thought she was going to be sick but she had to get it all out. *It's now or never.*

"After he beat me within an inch of my life, he turned his attention to my baby. He knew I wasn't going to fight him for myself. I had given up on me long ago. So, he went after the one thing he could get a rise out of me with. Holly." Carolynn gasped next to her, holding her hand over her mouth.

Annette began to rub her arms, trying to ease some of the chills she was feeling. "He wanted to punish me for this indiscretion that he concocted in his head. He picked Holly up by her nightdress and since she would not stop crying while he was yelling, he slapped her. He still cried even louder than."

A loud sob sounded in the room. Annette wasn't sure if it was from her or Carolynn, maybe even both of them. "My poor baby." Austin walked over to the counter and took her hand. Rubbing circles over her palms. Reassuring her enough to go on.

"He focused his attention on Holly. I was still on the floor, trying to get up from the pain, begging him to stop. She was screaming so loud and he couldn't handle the noise. I will never forget the words that came out of his mouth; they still bring bile to my throat."

She began to shake uncontrollably and Carolynn moved her chair closer to her. She took her other hand and rubbed her back. Mocking her ex-husbands' voice – "If you keep crying like that, I'll give you something to shut you up. Then he turned around to undo his pants. That moment of his back to us was my one chance. It gave me the time I needed to grab the fireplace poker and smash him over the head with it. I thought I had killed him at first and I felt happy about it. Actually happy. But it was short-lived. I had only given him a bad concussion with a gash. On top of that, I also gave him more rage toward Holly and me."

"Oh, you poor thing! Why is he not in jail?!" Carolynn pulled her in for a hug. Annette felt like she didn't deserve their sympathy. She pulled back from the other lady and wiped her cheeks.

He was in jail. All they convicted him of was assault because of what he did to me. They released him after a year for good behavior. PPPffft. Good behavior. Like what he did to me for years was good behavior? Ever since then I have been running. I keep a journal of every incident that has happened in my laptop bag. I get us somewhere that I think is far enough away and he still seems to find me. The restraining order against him never does any good. There is never a cop around when he gets to me, when he beats me, or when he tries to go after Holly!" She yelled that last part and emphasized it with her fist hitting the counter. It took her a few minutes to calm herself down. Trying to focus on her breathing. She had not been able to look at Austin the whole time. Not sure she could handle what she would see looking back at her.

"So now here we are. I was on the move again when you saw me at that diner. And it seems like he has found me once again, except this time I have no way to get away from him since he trashed my car."

"Do you have any family?" Even though she had turned her attention to Carolynn she noticed out of the corner of her eye Austin had taken the seat next to her.

"No. What was left of my family I had learned passed away in a house fire a year after Holly was born. I couldn't even make it to the funeral because of him. I have learned to rely on myself and to never stay anywhere too long. He always finds me." She blew out a long breath and wiped at her cheeks once more. "Wherever I go he shows up and causes more problems. If he finds me here, he'll not only bring his wrath on us but on you too. I don't want to have that kind of guilt on my conscience, and I understand if you want us to go."

"You're staying right here." It was Austin this time. The firmness in his voice caused her to turn to look at him. *He is giving me an order.*

"But I-."

"Not another word. You had your say and now it's my turn." She clamped her mouth shut. Relinquishing the conversation. A clock chimed from in the living room, filling the house's silence. Annette sat back in her seat and waited. "Now like I said you're staying here. Not only have I promised the sheriff I would keep an eye on you but I can't in my right mind allow for you to drag that little girl to God knows where. You're safer here then off on your own and I intend to keep t that way. There is no arguing this."

Annette grasped her hands together. Playing with her thumbs and sucking on her bottom lip. "I can't possibly intrude on you like this. Besides I need space in case something does happen. I don't want it on my conscience if Terry should find a reason to harm either or both of you."

"Oh Deary, it's not an intrusion. Not at all." Carolynn cooed the words to try and comfort her as well as herself. The elderly woman beside her making it so clear that they were welcome here and that made her smile.

"I am not used to being waited on. Plus, privacy is a big thing for me. I appreciate what you are trying to do but I can take care of us. I have been doing it for a long time. Now, I think I will just go find a place to rent until I can figure out what to do about my car." She pushed her chair back and stood. Carolynn following right behind her

.   "Austin don't just sit there, do something!"

He grunted under his breath and stood as well. Stepping in front of Annette blocking her path. He towered over her but not in a menacing way. "I do not see how you are going anywhere without me driving you." A smile tugged at the corner of his mouth. He thought he had won with that smug look on his face, but she wasn't going to make this easy. The more distance she put between him and her, the better.

"I don't need you to drive me. I have these things called legs and mine are not broke. In fact, they work perfectly well. I can walk." Crossing her arms in front of her she gave a smile of her own. Although her smile was more of a challenge.

Carolynn was looking back and forth between the two of them. Showing a knowing smirk of her own. She did not miss the sizzle in the air between them. It was not a challenge of wits but of pride, and possibly more.

He was the first to break eye contact. Cursing under his breath, Austin pushed his shoulders back, standing straight. Annette guessing, he was over six feet tall by how she had to tilt her chin so high to stare up at him. "You want to rent a room well you can have it, privacy and all right here." He held up his hand as she opened her mouth. "You can rent out the cottage we have outback. It's private and quiet. That way you get what you want and I am not breaking any promises. I told the sheriff you'd stay here and that's what I meant. Until they find him you aren't leaving and that's that. Besides, I couldn't live with *my* conscience if I just let you leave while he is still out there." He didn't omit that if she decided to leave he was required to call the sheriff to let him know, and his offer of her staying at the jail, for the time being, would still stand. He wanted her to make her own choice and hopefully, it was the right one.

Annette considered her options for a moment. She would have her peace and privacy if she left, and no one to tell her what to do. Although she had to admit the thought of leaving the man standing in her way brought a stab of pain to her heart. She knew she'd miss him after she left, heck she missed him now and he was standing inches away from her. Knowing he would be within yelling distance if she needed him was a comfort and reassurance she wouldn't have if she left. Going against her inner demons she nodded her agreement to stay.

The elderly woman became so delighted that she came around and wrapped her into a big hug again. This time following it with a kiss to the cheek.

"Oh, we will have to go over first thing in the morning and clear out all the dust! I am so happy you're staying! And don't worry about the rent dear. Just pay what you can when you can."

Austin left the room to go outside as the other woman fussed over her; making it clear the discussion was over. An ache filled her chest in his absence. What has she gotten herself into? Is this how it is going to be from now on? Will she always crave the look of him, the feel of him, his smell, and the mere presence of him? And what if something happened? *Maybe this is a mistake...*

****

The weather outside was cloudy, spitting rain down on him and the earth. It would seem the heavens felt as he did about all the information he had just received. Austin had never felt so much anger and sympathy for someone all at once before. Let alone someone he just met. What he had heard from her own mouth crushed his insides and made him ache with pain, and he hadn't even gone through it. Red hot rage coursed through him as she told her story. His hand a dull throb where he had crushed the glass. The heat of the day rising while the drops of rain kicked up the dust. Giving off a musky, sweaty atmosphere.

He couldn't imagine what it must have been like, how strong a person has to be to endure that treatment for so long. If there was one thing, he could make sure of was he wouldn't let anything further happen. If he had to go out and find the bastard himself and haul him in that's just what he'd do.

Not being able to sleep real long last night because he kept worrying, she was going to leave. He knew he was getting attached to her, but he wanted time to sort through it all and figure out what he wanted. Their conversation in the kitchen just now proved his thoughts were right. She was thinking of leaving. At least now he knew why.

He could not get the images of her body out of his mind. Gran could tell something was different this morning when he came down even earlier than usual. Although she never spoke about it. Instead, just asked him his thoughts on what to do next. He wanted to have gone back upstairs and taken her again but that would not have solved anything. He could still taste her, could still feel her shaking beneath him. A groan slipped from his lips and he rubbed the back of his neck. God, she was amazing last night. Letting go and giving all at the same time. *Those eyes looking up at him when she was on her knees! Stop!* This wasn't getting him anywhere and he had work to get done.

The rain had stopped but the clouds remained. Today was going to match his mood and thoughts appropriately. As he pushed the thoughts swimming around in his head away, he trudged his way to the barn. The sounds of nickering horses greeted him. The familiar scents of hay, straw, horses, and leather tickling his nose and calming his nerves. Nowhere else ever felt like home. He went through each stall checking their food and water. He checked over each mare and stallion he had in the barn to make sure no one was injured before letting them out to pasture. When he had to admit he had nothing else to work on that morning that would not be a challenge to focus on, he went to his truck. A drive would surely help clear his head.

He drove down the driveway swerving to miss the potholes, and onto the main road. Running over and over every detail in his head of what she had said. He couldn't understand how someone could do that to another human being, let alone a child. How sick someone had to be to even consider doing anything like that. Annette was so strong in his mind. Much stronger than anyone he knew, and he secretly admired her for overcoming so much and not giving up.

She had kept that child safe no matter what. Just remembering all the little chatter, he had shared with that little girl gave him a warm sensation in his stomach and brought a smile to his lips. He had grown very fond of both of them over the short time he has known them. They both made him wish to have a family and be a father, her father. *Whoa.* The admission shocked him so much that he pulled over to the side of the road and killed the engine. He wanted to be the one that little girl ran to for help. He wanted to call her his. H wanted to call them both his and he was stunned by this. People do not get this attached this quickly. It wasn't reality, but he could not deny he had been deeply affected by them. His logical mind couldn't believe it but his heart screamed the truth.

The more he thought about it, the more he realized he couldn't deny it. It was not just about Holly though. He wanted a family with Annette at his side. He had to figure out a way to get her to stay long enough to show her this would work. But how? Yes, he was attracted to her physically; there was no denying that, but he also felt the pull in his chest when he was around her. An emptiness when he wasn't. He knew something more meaningful could grow but he knew he had to give it time and not push too much. Already taking a gamble earlier today by challenging her to stay and he had been surprised she hadn't put up more of a fight. He would count that as a good sign. He was even more amazed that she hadn't run off when she looked like a deer in headlights telling her story. He gave a small chuckle under his breath when he thought about how his Gran reacted to her staying. So, delighted and cheerful.

Leaning his head back and closing his eyes after he rolled down the window. The breeze of the late afternoon brushing against his face. The air felt like a soft caress across his hardened features. He was going to have to figure out how to go about courting a lady. He hasn't been on a date in so long it seemed almost out of his depth. Courting, in general, was always awkward and Annette was no regular lady. She was going to take time to scale all the walls she puts up but he already knew it would be worth it. The summer breeze reminded him of her touch. Those fingers and soft skin rubbing up against him. To a hard-working ranchman, he always had the rough skin women sometimes complained about, but not Annette. No, she seemed to enjoy it. How soft she had been, almost afraid to touch him sometimes. Then it was as if a dam had broken and she just had to let out her emotions within her body. Groaning loud as his body reacted to the memory. His shaft straining against his jeans.

Hearing paper ruffling he opened his eyes. In the seat, next to him was her laptop in a satchel that had spilled some contents over his seat. The laptop was halfway out of the satchel, along with a book of some kind that was opening with the gust of wind from the window. He vaguely remembered Annette saying something about a journal. Something about recording things… events that had happened. With his curiosity peaked. His fingers itching to want to open and read about the horror that was her life. He wanted to understand where she had come from and her experiences. To get a glimpse of it all from her end. However, he also knew that by doing just that he'd be forcing an invisible wedge between them. If Annette ever found out he had read it without her then she might not trust him and if he learned anything about her he knew trust was hard to attain from her.

Yes, he wanted to know more about her, to have her open up to him so he can take some of her pain away, but he wanted her to tell him. He wanted her to want him to know. So instead of opening the pages of her past he closed his window, put the contents back into the satchel, turned his truck around and drove back towards home.

Chapter 7

Yesterday left a horrible uneasy feeling in the pit of Annette's stomach as she was woken up by Carolynn, telling her that her first appointment of the day was in an hour and she needed to get dressed ASAP. It was like a bad date that wouldn't end and no matter what she did to get out of it, she kept getting dragged right back in. Carolynn had insisted, after her caving in yesterday, that she had to make tons of appointments for her. "Somethings will need to be tended too," were her exact words. After a flurry of phone calls for a "proper" haircut, clothes shopping, new linens, and some groceries, because there were none in the cottage, even she felt exhausted. She was not invalid and she did not need to be babied. She was not expecting to even stay that long, however, she was being thrown into this.

Even after all that Carolynn had even pushed for Holly to enroll in preschool while they were here. Annette was not too fond of that idea due to her instability in one place. She did not want her daughter to get attached to one place only to have to pick up and leave. As soon as Austin left she had no time to herself. The other woman had her so frazzled and moving around that she had no time to even think.

She saw Austin once last night and that was as he ran upstairs to get a shower. Carolynn said he had a lot of work to get done and he would be eating his supper when he came in. So, we didn't wait up for him, but Annette got the feeling something else was going on and she just was not in on it. The unspoken words between them filled her thoughts as she washed

Holly and tucked her into bed. They even gave her a hard time going to sleep last night.

Either way, she was not going to worry over that this morning. She hauled herself out of bed and into a quick shower. Within the span of thirty minutes, she was out the door. A piece of toast in her mouth as she hurriedly buckled Holly into her car seat. She had no idea where she was going but she already conceded it didn't matter. Carolynn was going to get her to go one way or another and that was one stubborn woman she was not going to argue with.

Her daughter, on the other hand, was loving every minute of it. Reminding her of a McDonald's logo "I'm lovin it." Her endless chatter giving her a smile and filled her ears with a hint of normalcy. Finally feeling a hint of happiness for once and not wanting to disrupt it. Her daughter deserved a normal childhood with friends and family, even if it was a temporary situation.

Not noticing before, since it was dark and raining the night she pulled off the highway, but she drove right past a strip of buildings. It's not much of a town, just a few shops here and there but she quickly realized this is what their community revolved around. There were elderly ladies sitting on benches and couples mingling around what she would consider a sidewalk. Some of it was boards and some were cobblestones. Seemed like an odd mix of old ghost town meets middle ages. Carolynn informed her this is where you come to find out the local gossip. If this was the local gossip mill then none of them got out much. Carolynn pulled into a parking spot right in front of a stone building and Annette got out to get her daughter. Carolynn informed her that their first stop was the hair salon and walked towards the shop. Just as they entered the building her companion was greeted and pulled into a conversation by two other elderly ladies.

"Oh, Carolynn! Yoo Hoo!" The younger of the two hollered. She had grey thinning hair and was sitting in a rocking chair over by the hair dryers. They all approached, with Annette standing back a bit but still within hearing distance as the lady embraced her with a polite peck on the cheek. "You must tell us about your visitor. I hear she is an outlaw on the run."

"I heard she stole someone's child and they mean to put her in jail," the older woman commented from under the dryer. She was flipping through a magazine not looking at either woman as she talked.

Carolynn seemed surprised at the assumptions of these two women, "She has done nothing of the kind. You two always listen to everything you hear on the grapevine?" *There we go with the clicking sound.*

"Well no," The younger lady stated, "but Mrs. Flick said she heard it straight from the sheriff and that – "

"Mrs. Flick ain't nothing but a gossip starter and an obvious flake. Now you remember when she said she heard a whole heard of cattle had been eaten by ants and Mr. Jones was sleeping around on his wife because he had bought a shiny new diamond? When in fact he was renewing his wedding vows and those cows were being sent to the chop shop."

Both women nodded their heads in agreement. "Yes, well I guess you'd be right. Well, set us straight then. What is going on over there?" This time the lady under the hairdryer was looking up to pay attention.

Carolynn looked back at her then. Assessing in her eyes how much she should reveal. When she turned back around to the other ladies she merely smiled and said, "Well that is mostly the other ladies' business, but I will tell you this. She ain't running from the law, that precious child IS hers, and she is welcome to stay in my home anytime. She is a good person and I am mighty glad she chose to stay." The younger of the two didn't know what to say to that, so she dropped it. The elderly lady sat up a bit straighter and just kept prodding for more information.

"Well, what's your grandson think about this? He's living under a roof with a woman and her child with no connection to either one of 'em. I'd think an honest, God-fearing man like that would not want to deal with an unwed mother and another man's kid running around the house. Plus, didn't he just come back from ranching down in Texas? I heard he had his heartbroken."

Letting out a huff noticeable to anyone who was listening, although there were only about a handful of other patrons in the shop, she clasped her hands in front of her. Carolynn was not enjoying their conversation, that much she could tell, but she took it in stride. Annette had to give the other woman props.

"Well Evelyn, if you must know he seems to be enjoying their company just as much as they enjoy his. And yes, he just got back a month ago; however, you're going to have to ask him yourself about what happened. It is not my place to say."

The woman Carolynn referred to as Evelyn spoke again as she turned to walk away, "Anyhow, my granddaughter is coming to town for the festivities at the beginning of next month. She just graduated from law school and is coming to stay for a few weeks to recuperate from the stress. I think it would be nice if she and Austin met. Maybe I'll introduce her at the dance?"

Carolynn acted as though she didn't hear the other woman. She slowly walked to Annette and Holly and motioned to check them in at the counter. So many questions now spun around in her head about the man she thought she was getting to know, but obviously, she knew little about. It wasn't as though he shared a lot about himself anyway.

****

The sounds and the smells of the town were still lingering with her. Being introduced to so many people in a short amount of time really takes it out of you. She never would have imagined all the numerous amounts of people a tiny town like this could produce, she realized she would never remember anyone's name unless she was here a long time. Adding all the different appointments, no food yet and so much walking they had done she was plain whipped out. Even after all the gossip and judgments being made about her, and Carolynn trying to quash as many of them as possible, she really did start feeling like she could belong here. The pieces she always felt were missing seemed to be falling into place now for Holly and her.

Carolynn had gotten them new haircuts, took them grocery shopping, and clothes shopping. She had never felt so dotted on before that at first, she had been chastised by the other woman for staying silent and not accepting help. Eventfully though she gave in and allowed herself the small luxury of someone else taking care of her. Holly was a bit shy at first. Not being accustomed to handouts she shied away from the clothes rack not wanting to seem like she was asking for too much. But after Annette reassured her it was alright her darling daughter choose so many clothes, she would need another car to fit it all. She could tell the other woman, whom they were told to refer to as Gran now even though Annette was not comfortable doing that yet, was enjoying having someone to dote on.

While Carolynn took Holly to the potty Annette took the time to make a much-needed phone call to her editor and friend Roxanne.

The phone was picked up before the first ring ended. That could only mean she had been waiting by the phone. "Where have you been woman! I have been going crazy trying to reach you!" Her friend was yelling so loud she had to pull the phone away from her ear until the ringing stopped. Other patrons were starting to look at her. Probably wondering what all the noise was about. Annette just nodded to them, mouthed "I'm sorry" and turned around so her back was to them.

"Sorry, my phone was off and it hasn't been that great of a past couple of days." Annette took her time to fill Roxanne in on some of the details. Starting with the latest assault, the dinner, meeting Carolynn, to Austin, and finally what she was doing so far today. It wasn't easy trying to talk low with everyone behind her. She felt like she was under a microscope with all the other people staring at her. After she caught her breath from talking too fast, she realized Roxanne hadn't commented once. "What? Nothing to add?"

"Oh, I have questions, especially about this Austin fellow, but we have more pressing matters at hand. While you were unreachable, my office got raided. I knew it had something to do with you because all the perp too was Rolodex card with your information on it. Might I add, after trashing my office. My best guess is it would have to be your ex."

"A Rolodex? Really? What are you, stuck in the 1940s? No one uses them anymore." A playful smile running across Annette's face.

"You know I like my organization a certain way."

"Yes, we all know that. It is one of the reasons I like working with you."

"So, you leave my 1940's skill set alone. I will not 'get with the times' and you can't make me."

Annette could not resist egging her friend on, and Roxanne knew it. They loved going back and forth like this, and she truly needed to talk about other things. Things like this made her smile. It helped with all the worry in her heart to feel kid-like. "That would explain how he found me this time. Since you do not just keep your information on a protected computer file, like most normal people."

"Yes, well anyway at least you're ok. That's what matters. Hopefully, the police in the town you're in find him this time." She heard the clicking sounds of a keyboard in the background, "What is the name of the town where you're at? I forgot to ask." Clicking still resuming in the background.

Up until that moment she never realized she didn't even know where she was. Yes, she knew she was in Montana but she never knew the name of the town. "Well I am not quite- "

"Oh neverminded. Just shoot me an email with the address so I know where you are and where I can send you things." She missed the sound of her friend's voice. The ache of the familiar was touching the surface and making her get nostalgic. It was nice to know you have someone in your corner when it counts and Roxanne was that someone. "Now getting back to the task at hand, I need something in writing on your next book so I can present it to my boss. The upper management wanted a briefing on it last week, but as we all know these things never run on schedule. Unless that is you completed one for me…" Giggling filled her ears as she paused to answer. This usually meant that Roxanne had bought her more time because she knew it would not be done yet.

"I can get you the first three chapters and an outline of the book by tomorrow. That way they know what to expect and we both don't get into too much trouble. I don't need your head getting bitten off and I do not need them asking for my advance back." More giggling ensued. The easy banter that was so much a part of their friendship tugged at her heart and made it easier to smile. *How I missed this!*

"That would be great! I would need it by four so I can take it with me to my meeting tomorrow before the close of business. The book will need to be done by the end of the month. Do you think that is feasible?"

"Let's see. At the end of the month? That is just over two and a half weeks, away right? If I can focus without any distractions, maybe. I can't promise anything with everything that is going on, but I can try."

"As long as you're not playing around with Mr. Austin, I don't see how it will be a problem." The playfulness returning to her tone. Annette missed this. The times where she could just relax and have a fun conversation with someone. It revived her soul some to let go and just have fun. After a few more minutes and confirming her submission times, she said her goodbyes and hung up the phone.

She found Holly and Carolynn sitting at a table near the front of the dinner waiting for her so they could order their lunch. Sam came over to get their orders just as she had finished filling Carolynn in on her conversation with Roxanne.

Chapter 8

She had pulled out money from the ATM to give to Carolynn for the rental but the elderly lady told her she the first month's rent was free. She said Annette had a hard-few days and this would hopefully make things a bit easier for her. Annette didn't want to not pay for her share but grudgingly gave in when the other woman wouldn't budge on the subject. So instead, Annette paid for their lunch and a tank of gas for the trip back. Annette got the feeling that the other woman would not ask her for money at all just to keep her around longer.

She had never had a handout before and her first instinct was to argue, but thinking about how the other woman would feel about it she had given in. Maybe she was becoming too fond of this place and still on the fence about being here very long. She did not want to put these people in danger and getting attached could be dangerous. Even with Austin around the fact that her ex was still out looking for her made her feel trapped.

As they pulled into the pothole-filled driveway she noticed the newly polished sign hanging over the entrance. Studying it as they went under, she noticed the dark green paint and gold letters that read "Rayne Falls Ranch". "What's the story behind the sign? Does it stand for something?"

"Well, you see the ranch has been in our family for generations. Since 1702 when my ancestor Rayleen Trumpet married her husband, Baron McPherson. He was a farming and cattleman who fell in love with a Shoshone healer woman who took care of him when he became ill. At that time, she had been married to another man in her tribe, a warrior as the story goes. So as not to start conflict, Baron kept his love a secret; that is until he saw him beating her. The other members of the tribe either didn't know or looked the other way because she was his wife. Baron later found out it was because Rayleen had not barred any children for her husband yet. He defended her and would have lost his life if it wasn't for Rayleen. The warrior was going to go to his tent in the middle of the night and kill Baron, instead of wasting his time in battle he already knew he would win."

"Oh, that is horrible. So, what happened?"

Nodding her head in agreement, "Yes, it is. Thankfully Rayleen had informed Baron of this and he was prepared for the attack."

Becoming more intrigued with this story Annette sat up straighter in the seat, Holly napping in the back. "So why would Rayleen tell Baron if she knew it could mean a worse fate for her if anyone found out?"

"You see Rayleen was in love with Baron too. Unspoken, but very much shown with their actions. Later, the two men had fought but because of the knowledge of what was coming, Baron had the upper hand and defeated the Shoshone man. After receiving news of her slain husband, Rayleen left her tribe in search of her savior. The one who freed her of her pain. When she had found him, even though he had been hurt as well, he proposed his love to her and offered her a life with him. So, you see my Dear, even though life and love may be hard, in the end, it may all be worth the risk."

She thought that over for a minute, still a bit confused. "That still doesn't explain the name on the sign." The truck came to a stop next to a white van sitting in front of the house. The cooing sound of her daughter waking up in the back seat filled the cab.

"Well, Rayne was the nickname Baron had for her. Rayleen named the land Rayne falls because of when she fell out of pain and fell into love. She fell in spite of the risk." The other woman turned to look at the van then too. "I wonder what's going on around here?"

Both women got out of the truck at the same time, to see a very dirty Austin around the other side of the van hooking a tool belt around his waist. The sight of him without his shirt on and a sheen of sweat over his muscles made Annette's blood run hotter. She almost felt dizzy.

Holly ran up to him and he picked her right up. "Oh honey, he's busy and dirty. I'm sure he wants to be left to whatever he is doing."

"Oh, it's ok ma'am. She's only having a bit of fun. Besides, no dirt ever hurt anyone and I could use a break. Don't you two look mighty fine with your new do's." With the innocence of s child, Holly took that moment to wrap her arms around his neck to squeeze him and give his cheek a kiss.

Carolynn yelled over her shoulder that she was going in to start dinner. Noting that Austin should clean up before then. That woman was like a well-oiled machine to Annette. She never stopped and she always worked accordingly. Hearing the steps creak and the door shut behind her, she turned her attention back to the man holding her little girl.

Ignoring his last statement, "It seems as though she may have missed you." The reality of how this situation may affect her daughter when they inevitably had to leave, weighed heavily on her mind and gave her an uneasy feeling in the pit of her stomach. Her daughter had been through enough and she did not want to break her heart when they would have to leave. It is not like they could stay here forever, could they? No! Her mind was demanding her to put a stop to this, but her heart was not agreeing to it. Her heart longed for something else entirely.

"Well, I missed her too." Pulling Annette out of her thoughts for a moment, "I felt a bit lonely with only the horses and cows, and the voices in my head to keep me company." He was trying to crack a joke, she knew, but it wasn't making her feel much better. Holly giggled as he put her down but she saw the mirrored frown on his face that she knew she must be giving him. So, he didn't say anything else, just proceeded to follow Holly into the house.

The daylight outside was almost blinding. It had become increasingly more humid out since early that morning. The red barn seemed a huge contrast to the white house a mere twenty yards away. The fields all around them showing off their beauty in lush grass. Horses dotted the landscape in the distance and trees loomed far off in their pasture. Obviously for the pure reason of providing shade on days like these.

She could almost see herself waking up to this every day. To know that none of this scenery would ever change, but grow better with age. Being able to let Holly roam and get into mischief like regular kids, but it was all a fantasy. A dangerous fantasy since she had to keep her mind on much more serious matters. She would never be able to enjoy any of it anyway. There wasn't a time she could remember when she wasn't looking over her shoulder, or being able to relax enough to completely fall sleep without feeling like she may have to jump up at any moment and flee.

So lost in her thoughts she didn't even hear him walk up behind her, but she felt his presence before he spoke. "A beautiful sight."

"Oh. Yes, the land is beautiful." With her emotions so unchecked she did not risk turning around to face him. She was afraid that she'd want to jump on him and kiss him senseless. To beg for him to take her fears away and chase all her demons away. That would seem too silly of a thing to say to a man she barely knew but felt like she had known for decades. He would think she is mad, and to open up so much to a person whom she may not see again would be pointless. The irony of wanting a man, without really knowing him, only to know you can never have him is like willingly putting myself in a box with no air because I like the box. I know it is not going to last, but still wanting it is selfish of my own sanity and safety of everyone.

Straining to hear him, he said it so low but what came out of his mouth sent little sweet shivers throughout her body. "I wasn't talking about the land."

He placed his hands on her shoulders. He was so close behind her that when she turned around her cheek brushed his bare arm. She looked up into his eyes and saw what she was afraid of. He wanted her, his eyes practically begging. Her lips slightly parted at the havoc he was causing to her sense and he must have taken that for an invitation. His mouth covered hers with such raw need that she pressed back into him just as fiercely. The hands that were still holding her shoulders dug in a bit deeper as his need grew. He pulled her to his chest deviling deeper into her mouth with his prodding tongue. When a moan escaped her, he groaned and pulled her away from him.

Even with him breaking all contact, her head was still swimming from the onslaught of sensations he brought in her. She began to sway a little. His hands on her shoulders were the only thing keeping her up. She was sure she would have collapsed I a pile of goo on the dirt ground. "I'm sorry. I shouldn't have done that." A slap to the face could not have hurt her more than those words did at that moment. How dare he turn her on within an inch of her sanity, making her want him ferociously, just to take it all away in an instant just because of what?! Having a guilty conscience? Being gentlemanly? Or pure morale? Either way, she was not going to give him the satisfaction.

"No need to be sorry. I deserved that. You gave me what I needed right? So, no need to be sorry." She knew she was pushing buttons just from the display of emotions that flew across his face, but she didn't care. He had caused her to feel bad about something that made her feel good. Made her feel wanted.

He considered her eyes and stepped back from her. Assessing that it would be better for him not to comment on whatever that remark was about, he let it be. "Gran told me that I am to help take your bags into the house. But I think it would be better to help take them into your new place instead." Annette gave him a curious stare. "I decided early this morning that the cottage could use a bit of sprucing up so I took it upon myself to clear it out. Besides, Gran isn't as fast as she tries to make herself these days and I didn't need her straining herself out over something she wouldn't have been able to do anyway."

He walked over to the truck and pulled Holly's and her bags out. Without saying another word, he strode away. Since he was much taller than her mere five feet three inches, she had to power walk to catch up to him. She had just matched his stride when they came around the back of the house. She saw a gravel driveway dotted with cherry trees. Following about another thirty feet or so was a lovely grey cottage with a white trimmed porch, windows, and door.

****

Taking all morning to make the place homier for a mother and small child, sweating his ass off fixing things and painting, was all well worth it to see the look on her face. She stood there staring for a few minutes, rubbing her eyes a few times. He wasn't sure if she couldn't believe it or if she was holding back tears. Either way, she looked so beautiful to him just standing there with pieces of her hair falling around her face. She may not know it, but she had a pure prepossessing nature about her that pulled at him. The strands were hypnotizing in their swaying. He wanted to grab a handful and tug on them. He wanted her. He knew it as soon as he saw her get out of the truck. Heck, he'd been thinking about her all day. And if the hard-on he had was any indication then he knew he shouldn't follow her in that house. Hell, he knew he shouldn't have kissed her a few moments ago but his body and his mind were not agreeing on a lot lately.

Every minute he spent in her company was killing him because all he wanted to do was take her in his arms and make love to her. However bad he wanted it, he knew she didn't need that right now. Whether or not she knew it herself, he knew she needed stability and reassurance that he wouldn't stand by and let her run away again. She needed a solider. A rock. Someone who would move mountains and slay beasts for her. He wanted her to believe that she had a family here, a future here, with him.

"Be careful of everything white. The paint won't dry until tomorrow." He said as they reached the steps. He noticed her eyeing the rocking chairs and swing, so he had to make sure she wouldn't sit on them too soon. She held the door open for him and followed him inside when he passed. The cozy Livingroom was furnished. In fact, the whole house was furnished, but prior to this morning, it had items in it from decades ago. He had ordered all new furniture online from the local homes good store, Rubies in the Rough. Mostly everything was pine wood. Other items included a flat-screen TV, sheer white and green curtains to match the green paint on the walls and the white couch. It also had two end tables and a coffee table. "Sorry about the smell. I left all the windows open to air it out. It should be gone by tomorrow." Placing the bags down on the floor he watched her as she slowly walked around the room, touching everything she could. "There is no carpets. Gran had them removed a few years ago. So all the floor is hardwood and re-sanded. The bedrooms though do have area rugs." He couldn't gauge how she was feeling since she was looking everywhere but at him.

She finally looked up at him and blushed, making him want to kiss her again. *Be still my heart.* "I'm sorry. I'm just not used to having anything this nice, let alone done for me. I am used to hotels, or dinners, or my car. Sometimes a crappy rental till I have to move on. I guess I just feel like I'm in a storybook."

His hear contracted a few times before he was able to get any words out. When he finally could speak, the words seemed so hollow compared to what he truly felt. "It just takes getting used to. I am sure you'll feel right at home soon." *Could I be any more generic?!* "If you'll follow me you'll see I cleared out and made up the kitchen for you." Not skipping a beat as he walked through the arched doorway that leads to the kitchen, "The kitchen had been redone a few months ago when Gran wanted renovations to freshen up the old place. All I did was clear out some cabinets and brought in a nice table set for you. There isn't a ton of room for a big table, as you can see, but enough for you and Holly. This nook is where Gran used to put her plants."

He knew he was rambling but he just couldn't help it. She made him feel so many emotions which made him uneasy right now. His need to please her out weighting all of them at the moment. The need to do or be anything for her growing with every breath. *Please make her happy so she will stay*. Repeating the same actions from the other room, where all she did was touch every surface, he noticed must be a thought process for her. She seemed to be weighing everything in her mind. Taking it in. She hadn't said one thing for a while as she was walking around the room, that he thought she might just want to leave. Coming a full circle around the kitchen she finally stood right next to him, making it a point not to look at him but out the glass doors that led to an enclosed porch.

"That porch," trying to get her to talk, "only has a couch on it for now, but if you'd like to put something else in there just let me know. I'll pick it up for you." She glanced at him and then back outside again. "Or you could order it. It's no big deal one way or the other. It's fully insulated so you can use it any time of the year." Was she trying to torcher him by making him wonder what she was thinking?

She nodded to his words but didn't turn or comment. The rest of the tour through the cottage she kept silent. They viewed the rest of the main floor. It included a den with a desk and some bookcases, and a half bath. They walked up the stairs at the front door to inspect the two nicely laid out bedrooms and hall bathroom. Austin had made it a point to furnish it kid-friendly. He adored Holly's room with a purple toddler bed, purple dresser, white lamps, pink toy chest, and a few toys. The walls he painted a light shade of pale lilac on two walls and the other two a pale pink to match. The bathroom he ordered some light green rugs, towels, and a hamper. When it came to Annette's bedroom, he had called the store to get advice from a saleswoman.

The woman picked out an emerald green for her bedding and curtains, so Austin decided to paint her room a pale green to match. He had the movers arrange al the furniture in the room, thinking it might be a bit to assuming and intimate to do it himself. The two rooms were such a contrast to one another but fit them perfectly well, in his opinion.

When they had finished their tour in her bedroom, Annette walked over to him and wrapped her arms around his neck. Completely caught off guard, it took him a moment to wrap his arms around her waist. Neither one of them moved except when Annette nuzzled her face against his shoulder. He felt his shoulder and chest starting to get damp, and he knew she was crying. Hushing her lightly as he stroked his fingers through her hair. She smelled so good. Too good. Her arms fell to her sides but she didn't pull away. She just leaned into him and let him hold her. He lifted her chin just as she began to speak, "I'm sorry. I know I have been apologizing a lot lately, but I shouldn't have…" He kissed her. This wasn't a lust-driven kiss. This was a kiss of promises to come, of blending together, of comfort, and of so much more than either of them could say. A tenderness they had both been without for so long.

Chapter 9

He felt so right pressed against her. He placed both hands to her cheeks, holding her still as he urged her mouth open with his tongue. Willfully opening to him, he caressed the softness of her mouth; exploring every inch. Annette moaned, at least she thought that was her. She couldn't be sure if the noise came just from her. It couldn't have been more cliché, and she certainly would not say it out loud, but just the thought of it made her smile inside. They blended together, she felt it, just as easily as rainbows colors blend into one.

They slowly moved together against the wall. Her hands came up to rest on his arms that were still cradling her face in his hands. Him leaning further against her, made her heart race. She could feel every outline of muscle in his chest and thighs. Knew the moment he got increasingly more solid against her. Her eyes fluttered closed as he began trailing kisses down her neck. His hands burning a similar pattern down her until he got to the dip in her top. As he licked the peak of each breast, he eagerly cupped her in his palms.

"You're so beautiful." His voice becoming more horse with every word, "I could taste you all day." Annette couldn't believe the effect he was having on her. This was all happening so fast, too fast, that her nerves were all tangled up. Her heart pounding in her chest and her clit was pulsing so bad she knew just one firm touch from him on her tight little nub would send her over the edge. Rubbing against him seeking release proved to be fruitless. But

she was enjoying every second of it and from the feel
of him, she would say he was too.

The feeling of pain, heartache and the thoughts
of fear melted away with every stroke, every embrace,
and every tingling caress of breath on her skin. That
husky chuckled came from his sweet lips, "Is this my
shirt?" She returned his question with a shrug, "Yes, it
is. You said it looked better on me anyway." He
looked at her then, fondling her with his eyes as he
began to unfasten the buttons. Slowly. One by one,
still staring into her eyes. "It will look so much better
if it was on the floor."

Annette felt a rush of heat between her legs
that she felt them shake. Her breath caught in her
throat. The image of him wearing this shirt against all
those muscles splashed across her eyes and made her
moan again. Oh yes! "Tell me what you want
darling."

She was going to tell him she wanted him to
take her to bed and make love to her, but before she
could reply a sound from downstairs flew her eyes
open. He must have heard it too because he jumped up
and backed away. Annette quickly re-buttoned her
shirt and simultaneously fixed her hair.

We heard a clink of something in the living
room then, "Anyone up there?" as Carolynn yells up
the stairs.

"Yea Gran. We'll be right down." He turned to
her and said, "We will finish this later." With that, he
walked down the stairs whistling. Whistling! What did
he have to whistle about!?

Walking down the stairs brought back bygone
memories from when she was a teenager and she had
just been caught necking in her room with the door

closed. Even though they were both grownups and it was perfectly okay to do, it didn't change the fact that her face began to get hot as a blush crept into her cheeks. Carolynn obviously noticed because she came up to her and helped her walk down the last few steps patting her hand as she went.

"Oh, you poor dear, the heat must be pretty bad upstairs. Well now, let's just get that AC on and we will have this house all nice, and cozy for you." Annette silently thanked higher beings for the fact that the other lady could not read minds.

Austin knowingly smiled at her as he walked over to the thermostat and turned it down a few degrees. She doubted the change in temperature was going to help the heat she was feeling. She would need to take a cold shower after this. Before they both left Carolynn had informed her that her daughter was playing with a deck of cards on the back sunroom, and Austin told her he had placed her laptop and a book on the kitchen table.

Getting used to her surroundings was easier than she thought. It was almost as if she had always lived there, it was a silly notion. However, she knew where everything was at the first shot. Every drawer she opened was correct. The utensils, plates, cups, and even the trashcan that was built under the counter. This could have been her I another life, she was almost certain of it. She watched as her daughter played with the deck of cards through the sliding doors to the sunroom.

She proceeded to make a simple supper of soup with veggies since the pantry had been stocked for her. She took a few seconds while the soup was heating up to send an email to Roxanne. It was nice of

Austin to leave a sticky note with the wireless login information for her to use. Seems he went and set it all up on his own for her. She reminded herself to thank him later. When she was done Holly and she sat down to eat.

"So, honey, what do you think of the place?" She tried to start up a conversation because Holly hadn't said one word since they sat down. "Do you like it here?"

No reply but her daughter nodded her head. Something was off, but she wasn't sure if it was her being tired or if it was her upset about something else.

"You ok munchkin? Is something bothering you? Do you not want to be here?" Annette couldn't help herself but she had to know what had her daughter so upset.

"Mommy,"

"Yes, pumpkin?"

"Do you think we can stay here for a while?" Her daughter looked up at her with big eyes rimmed with tears and it about broke her heart in pieces.

"Would you like to stay?"

Holly just pushed her soup around with her spoon. Not touching a bite of it. She looked back down at her bowl, "Do you think he will find us here? Mr. Stin is nice. I wike it here and everyone is nice."

Annette knew who he was. Her father. She didn't want to lie to her but she needed her daughter to feel safe. She knew that sooner or later it would get to her, but she was hoping it wouldn't be till later. Taking a deep breath, "I like it here to baby. I don't know if he will find us here, but I do know we are with people who care about us." Wow, she couldn't believe that she really said that. It felt strange to have someone who you know will think about you if or when they would leave. She had never had that before. "Now, if you finish your soup we will go look at your room before bath time."

That perked her right up. She sat up straighter and started devouring her food. A smile at the corner of her mouth. Annette knew her daughter was worried, but she would rather that all the worry away from her. It was a burden no child or liable and responsible parent should have to deal with. Sometimes the system worked against people rather than helped them and this was one of those times.

Holly's face lit up like Rudolph the red-nosed reindeer when he finally got to lead Santa's sleigh. She ran around touching everything in her room. Pulling almost everything out so she could look at it and lots of squealing. It wore Anette out just to experience it through her. She could not imagine how worn out Holly was after her excitement dulled down. With now real nap and a long day of running around, it seemed to be getting the better of her. So, before she got her ready for her bath before anything else happened.

Watching her daughter take a bath in their new bathroom, blowing bubbles everywhere, she couldn't grasp how they came to this. Bubbles filled her strawberry blonde hair and made her giggle when they got in her nose. The sound filled Annette's heart full of bliss. A few days ago, she wouldn't have believed anyone if they told her she would be living in a place like this, with people like the McPherson's who cared about them, and a man who stirred so many emotions in her that she wanted to give him her trust. She wanted to give him her heart.

She already knew her daughter adored him. It was obvious. Annette had always been really careful when it came to her daughter, she never wanted to put her in a bad situation. She feared though that by doing that she had been sheltering her from life itself. She needed to get out more with other kids and be a child, and Annette was feeling like this would be the perfect place to do just that.

****

After two weeks of nothing but working on her book, taking care of Holly, drudging back and forth between her feelings for Austin, and her fear of the inevitable she was exhausted. Mentally and physically. Annette had not been able to sleep longer than two hours, and that was when she could sleep. She felt lonely during the day and found horror in her dreams. She did find solace out on the porch on nice days and playing with her daughter when she took some time off from writing. Carolynn had been wonderful in helping her with her daughter, telling her that she had no great-grandkids yet and it was nice having some youngins to fuss over. Besides Holly was having the time of her life. She got spoiled with all the attention that a kid should get from a great grandmother figure. Something her daughter would never get from her own family.

Sheriff Townsend came by a few times with no new leads. They had tracked some sittings, but nothing was confirmed. From what he thinks her ex could have moved onto another town. Since this one is so small, normally people would have noticed a newcomer in town. He lifted the ban on leaving since she had taken up residence. He was still going to check in on her from time to time to make sure nothing new has happened. He genuinely seemed worried about their safety and had an almost brotherly concern for finding her ex.

This helped Annette relax more in his presence, knowing he already read her previous reports and knew what they were all up against. She also felt herself confiding in Sheriff Townsend about the incident she had not reported, just to make sure she got an account of everything. She felt the pride of his uniform when he puffed up his chest more and responded with, "We will catch him. One way or another ma'am." She never mentioned how catching him wasn't the problem. Keeping him and stopping him was.

Annette had to figure out other ways to pay her rent to the other lady. Neither Carolynn or Austin would allow her to pay any monetary value towards her staying there. So instead, she had to get more creative. She had paid for groceries, paid for the plumber who came out to fix the bathroom sink in the main house, and her latest was paying to have the driveway repaved. That one was a big surprise to Carolynn and Austin since it was expensive. The driveway was in horrible shape and very long. The expense did not surprise her thought when she found out it had never been done since it was first paved over the dirt drive. As anyone could imagine, it sorely needed it. Austin had tried to talk her out of it, saying she didn't need to do it, but she felt it was the least she could do. The process is still in the early phase as they had to pull up the old driveway, mark it out, and then flatten the pad underneath.

Carolynn had discussed plans with her and the two ladies came up with a long circular drive where the house was, and an extra pad over by the barn. Making it easier to access if it rains or snows too much. Anette had not told Carolynn, but she was making sure to add a surprise design element to complete the look. She was so excited about it that sometimes she felt like she would blurt it out. It was hard to keep a secret when she knew she was actually making someone else happy.

The other woman told Annette in confidence about Austin's parents who had passed in a tractor-trailer accident. Austin, the eldest of three, was only nine when it happened. Carolynn said he had taken on the responsibility of being a man real young because there were no other male figures around. Her own husband had died a year before Austin's parents from a heart attack, so the only other men were the ranch hands and they just couldn't be bothered much. None of them wanted to waste time with a broken kid so she took on the role of mother, grandmother, and male role model. It was tough, but she felt like he tuned out good. Annette couldn't agree more.

The wind blew across the open fields, brushing against the grass creating ripples that reminded her of water. Clouds lazily swept the sky and birds began to dot the scenery. Hearing the nickering of horses in the pasture out front of the main house brought her attention that way.

She hadn't seen Austin much these past two weeks. It was as if he was spacing himself from her. Since the almost incident in her bedroom that first day she moved in she could tell he had pulled back from her, but she couldn't tell why. As she followed the cobblestone pathway around the side of the main house she could see a shadow figure of him on his horse, a black appaloosa stallion that she had been told was named Solitaire. He couldn't see her from that distance but Annette could swear she felt his eyes on her. She began to get goosebumps on her arms with the feelings it invoked within her.

She quickly hurried up the steps and through the front door. Carolynn was expecting her for an early dinner. Holly had already run over after lunch to help out. The dinner was to celebrate the finishing of her book and Annette didn't want to keep them waiting. As soon as she came into the kitchen she was handed a bag.

"What's all this for?" Holly was already busy standing on a step stool tossing a salad next to Carolynn. Her daughter being so caught up in what she was doing didn't even acknowledge her.

"Those my dear are potatoes that I need you to peel for me. I am going to boil them for mash taters." She turned to put a small trash can on the counter. "This is for the peels. The peeler is in the bag. Now get going."

Every spud she took out and peeled was so natural. The movements, the soft chitchat that went around the room, the smiles and the silence between them at times. All of it felt right somehow and made her wonder if this is what it would feel like to have a family. Tears ached at the back of her eyes and she realized she was experiencing joy for the first time I a long time. This is what was missing from their lives, the smile on her daughter's face was evidence enough, and she was never-ending grateful for this woman who had given her so much hope.

Having to clear her throat before she could talk, "This is a lot of food for just us. Are you expecting more company?"

Moving with fluid motion between the oven and fridge, grabbing ingredients to put in her pot on the stove. "Yes and no. I want to make enough for when Austin comes back in from out in the field. That poor boys' been working too hard lately. Seems to me he's trying to get his mind off of something." Not saying a thing, Annette just put her head down and focused on her task.

Carolynn was still moving back and forth when she continued, "And what do you think that might be?"

Holly finished what she was doing and started making a pee-pee dance on the stool. "Honey do you have to go potty?" Both of them knowing she was avoiding the question. "Yes, mommy." Holly rushed down the step stool and down the hallway towards the bathroom. When the bathroom door closed Annette focused her attention back onto what she was doing. Carolynn had already finished checking her food and came over to help peel the potatoes.

While they were alone Carolynn started a conversation, Annette wasn't sure she was ready for. "Annette, I want to talk to you. Woman to woman. I would have to be blind not to see the sparks that shoot between my great-grandson and you. "Holly took that moment to bound back into the kitchen with a satisfied grin on her face. Kneeling down to talk to her daughter, "I see you finished." Holly feverishly nodded her head in proud accomplishment. "Why don't you take your juice box and go watch some cartoons."

Holly didn't wait another second. She grabbed her juice box off the counter and went into the Livingroom. Soon music faded into the kitchen from one of her daughter's favorite cartoons. Going back to the seamless rhythm of peeling potatoes she knew the other woman wanted to continue their conversation. Annette took a deep breath and looked up at her, waiting.

Carolynn started off slowly, "I am only asking this for both your sakes. I don't want to see him in pain, and I have become fond of you too. So, I would like for neither of you to have to hurt. Carolynn stopped peeling to pull out a chair and sit down. Leaving Annette still standing to look down at her. She liked this woman and did not want to cause issues for her. That is the whole reason she didn't want to stay in the first place. A choice that sometimes gave her pangs of anxiety and made her think she may have made a mistake in staying.

After starting to peel again, "What I want to know is your overall intentions towards Austin. He hasn't had an easy time with life, let alone relationships, and I just want to make sure where your heart stands on the matter? I know it is not my place to ask but I am generally concerned for both of you."

Annette didn't want to lie to her, nor could she give an answer that she wasn't sure of yet. So, she settled for what she could tell her. "I honestly am not sure what is going on. My life right now is not one hundred percent stable. Do I like him? Absolutely. There's no doubt in my mind that it could be so much more, however, he has been shying away from me for the last few weeks." Annette stopping what she was doing to look directly at her, "You alone have made this part in both our lives memorable. You both have impacted mine and Holly's lives in so many ways. I am so grateful for it. But right now, until I can get things straightened out with Terry, and make sure I will not have to leave again, I can't say what I want because it might end abruptly. My feelings need to be put on hold and what Holly needs will always come first." Annette went back to peeling her potatoes.

All Carolynn did was listen, not interrupting once. She nodded her head a few times, while still peeling potatoes, ad when Annette had finished talking she began clucking her tongue again.

"I hear what you are saying, I do. I can understand and respect your need to do what is necessary for your daughter. What I see though is a scarred little girl trying to keep her world from falling apart. You have become part of this ranch. There is no denying it. From the first moment, I saw you in that booth, I knew you could change our lives as much as we can change yours. I still believe that. I consider you family, whether you are kin or not. That little girl in there has brought so much joy to us that we couldn't dream of her, or you for that matter, just getting up and leaving. So as far as I am concerned, there will be no more talk about that. Understood?"

"But I- "

Carolynn held up her hand, "Now listen, I don't want to hear of you leaving again. You *ARE* safe here. You need to believe that before that little girl can believe it. If you being here this long doesn't prove it then I don't know what will. Besides, out there you have no one. Here you have family, at least I hope you consider us as such. She scooted the chair back and stood, placing her last peeled potatoes in the bag. "Look I don't know what's going through that head of his, but give him time. You of all people should know how hard it is to trust people. He just needs someone to prove they are worthy of it. "

There was one thought she couldn't get out of her head. A question that she felt would shine more light into who Austin is. "What happened to him in Texas? I heard he had a girlfriend. Where is she now?' The question gnawing at her like a dog chews on a bone.

"Only he can explain that to you. Maybe you should ask him."

"Should ask who? Him? What?" Both women jumped at the voice in the doorway, letting out tiny screams of alarm. Annette's hand flying to her chest to calm her pounding heart.

"Austin, you scared us half to death! Don't do that again! You're worse than a child sneaking around on Christmas morning, sneaking upon us." Carolynn threw her rag at him. Annette didn't even turn around to see. Little shivers trailing up her spine when she sensed his eyes on her. *God, would this affect ever stop*? "Go get a shower and leave us to finish up. Dinner will be ready in thirty minutes."

When Anette caught her bearings, she stood to go into the Livingroom. Their eyes locked as she was walking past and he spoke, "Good. I'm starving." She hoped he didn't see her shudder at the lust in his eyes at the double meaning. Knowing the innuendo was meant for her she immediately got more excited. Just the thought of his mouth on her, tasting her, made her panties wet.

Chapter 10

Austin climbed the stairs with a purpose. His body has been feeling the effects of lack of sleep and throwing himself into running the ranch. Turing out the herds, vaccinations, fixing the milking machines, tagging the meat cows and the calves were all just distractions. All things he had more time to do but got done in less time than normal just to avoid a woman who was driving his mind crazy. He had decided to give her some space. That look in her eyes when they had almost been caught showed him how ready she was to run. He felt how her muscles contracted and sensed her anxiety. Truth be told, he couldn't lie about how fast he was falling for her and how quickly they had escalated their – he didn't know what kind of relationship this was.

They never discussed anything about the future If he had to guess, she had never thought about having one. He needed time to think about jumping into a relationship with a woman who wasn't sure if she wanted to be in one. He already had his emotions toyed with before, he wasn't sure he wanted to go through that again.

As the sprays of hot water from the shower ran down his back he closed his eyes. Remembering his time away from the ranch in Texas always put him in a sullen mood. His sense of morals didn't seem to apply to everyone and when that harsh reality set in he knew he was in the wrong place. The hot water started helping his muscles to relax. Bones and joints cracking from the release and he flexed to try to relieve some more tension. He began to wash off, making sure he got all the grit off of him from the day and ran some shampoo through his hair- all the while thinking of the shiver that he saw run through Annette's body earlier.

He began to get aroused at the thought and inwardly groaned. That woman does something fierce to him. Her body was so soft and lush he couldn't remember ever reacting to a woman so fiercely. He had had women before but never anything like this. She pulled at him, made him want to protect her and provide for her which also was a bit off-putting at times. She was independent, proud, and so very hurt and scared that it sent him in so many directions.

He blew out a breath, leaning on the wall after making the water even hotter. He welcomed the sting of the shower to ease his mind. After a few moments, he decided his erection was not going to go away any time soon so he turned the water as cold as he could get it. Wincing from the sudden change and clearing his mind until his body relaxed enough for him to recover. He turned the shower off and got out to dry off. He had just wrapped a towel around his waist when a knock sounded on the door.

He opened it expecting to see his Gran but it was Annette standing there with her mouth open staring at him. He threaded fingers through his wet hair and smiled at her. She recovered quickly, but not quickly enough. He saw the way she looked him over and stopped at the towel. He cleared his throat and she shot her eyes back up to meet his.

"Oh. I was just… I was to tell you dinner is ready." He loved the smooth lines of her neck as she swallowed. Those eyes that saw into him without even noticing. He knew he was getting hard again and it was confirmed by her gaze dropping again.

"Is there something else you came up here for?" The blush that crept up her neck and the way she licked her lips when her eyes crept back up to his was so beautiful and sexy that he almost grabbed her to bring her into his room. He knew if he did that they would take up way too much time and they would surely be missed downstairs. He couldn't make out the light whisper that came from her but in an instant, she turned and all but ran down the hallway. He smiled again as he closed the door and started to get dressed. At least he knew she still wanted him as much as he wants her. He just hoped they could grow on it.

****

Dinner was a nice peaceful occasion. Austin had congratulated her after coming back downstairs. She hardly got out a thank you as she stood there assessing him while remembering their exchange a few moments ago. She knew she was openly staring at him but she couldn't help herself. He was downright gorgeous and all masculine in his damp hair, tight grey shirt, and form-fitting blue jeans. They hugged his hips and ass so well she wished she was a part of them. His bare feet showed her how far down his tan really went.

The two women were sitting at the dining room table chatting about their day when he had walked in and took a seat. Annette tore her eyes away from the hunky specimen to continue feeding her daughter. They chatted a bit about her book and things that still needed to be done on the ranch. She was glad he never asked about the topic he had walked in on of her and the other woman talking about earlier. Instead, he stuck to talking about the ranch which suited her just fine. He noted he had replaced some fencing and bought more cattle for the south pasture. He wanted to be ready when the calving season started and may need to look into hiring two more hands. One of the mares was about ready to give birth soon and he had heard one of the other ranches had a horse stolen yesterday. Austin must have sensed Annette's tension because his eyes darted to hers when he relayed that information.

"You shouldn't be worried about it. If it was your ex well find him." He almost growled the 'Your ex' part and she knew he hated saying it, she couldn't understand why though. It wasn't like she cared about the bastard. "Ranchers don't take too kindly to their stock being stolen. If it was him, he could have done it to move around this landscape faster, that still doesn't mean he would take into account the variations of wildlife on these lands. That alone could give him problems." He said before stabbing into a slice of his steak.

"It also could be poachers taking the horse or another person taking a horse. An animal might have gotten it too. We are not positive it was Terry. He hasn't been heard from or seen in weeks. Maybe he moved on." He put the food in his mouth. Being grateful for the man sitting there trying to make her feel better. She knew he was only trying to calm her down but Annette also knew better.

Annette wanted to be hopeful, she really did but the more she thought of hi moving around undetected the more spooked she got. She put down the fork when Holly was done eating. Holly wanted to go watch more TV but Annette told her she needed to wash her hands and face off first. Carolynn shooed her to sit back down when Holly ran down the hallway to the restroom. "You haven't eaten a thing all day. I think you're losing too much weight overall this stressing. I will take her to wash up, and I don't want any of my food going to waste." The woman turned to look at Austin, pointing a finger at him. "You make sure she cleans her plate while I am gone." With a huff, she scooted down the hall after her daughter.

Austin gave her a tiny scowl and she turned her eyes down to her plate. "What does she mean you haven't been eating?" Embarrassment shot through her turning her to the defensive. Taking her eyes off the plate in front of her she shot him her own look of annoyance. "She just said I haven't eaten today", sidestepping the question and hurrying on, "you haven't been around much lately. You been eating all your meals?" He frowned with that and looked almost apologetic. Not being able to stand it she looked back down at her plate. She hadn't been worried about eating lately. She was worried about Holly and finishing her book. She wanted to stay here but the problems seem to be starting up again. She knew the horse being stolen, no matter how much she didn't want it to be, was Terry. It was just one horse. That in itself sent alarm bells off in her mind. She was just about to bring up the topic of her leaving again when Austin spoke up.

"If this is going to be a safety issue for you and you are too stressed we can always put in safeguards." She looked up at him. Holding back the tears in her eyes.

"What do you mean?" Giving him a quizzical look.

He used a spoon to point at her plate. Gesturing she should take a bite. She got the feeling he wouldn't continue till he saw her eat something. After she made a big show of stabbing her steak and taking a big piece into her mouth he continued. "Like an alarm system or we could get you a dog? You could always move back into the main house again too." He frowned at her when she didn't answer him. "The very least we could work with Holly on an escape route. I know she is young but this way if anything does happen she will have her own way of getting to safety too."

Annette wasn't sure about getting a dog. Dog's meant responsibility and that meant sticking around. She wouldn't mind an alarm system though. Not being real sure the escape plan would work or if it wouldn't taint her daughter's psyche in the future she shook her head. She wasn't positive this would be the best way to resolve her fears

Austin mumbled something under his breath just as she heard Carolynn in the kitchen talking to Holly. The woman was chastising the little girl for tricking her into getting her cookies but Annette could tell she was playing with her. Carolynn yelled in the other room, "You two eating that food in there?" They both replied with yes in unison and she chuckled. Holly rushed in with cookies filling both her hands. "Look what I have mommy!" The other woman following behind almost panting but smiling. "That one is a spitfire if I ever saw one. She won't stop talking till you give in. She better be a lawyer someday with how she talked me into giving her those treats."

Austin and Annette laughed before Holly dashed into the Livingroom, a smiling Carolynn behind her. Austin got up and moved to the seat Holly had been in. He picked up her spoon and filled it with mashed potatoes. He smiled at her and told her to open up. He slowly fed her a few spoonful's. Staring into her eyes the whole time. What felt like an hour was probably on a minute or two, but it was so intimate that she wanted to look away. She was going to protest to him feeding her but he put the spoon on the table before she could.

He grabbed a napkin to wipe at her mouth. "Now, what other options, other than moving, do you have? And FYI you are not moving. That is final. Besides Holly has a right to as much of a childhood as she can get. That means dealing with the situation as best as she can too." Even though she was glaring at him, she did have to admit if nothing else he was a hard ass. *Yea, a hard ass that steals your breath and makes you weak in the knees.* Without saying a word, she nodded. He was right and she couldn't see any harm in allowing Holly to feel more empowered. If anything, it would mean he would be around more and that would give them more chances to get to spend time together. Images of his hands on her made her all tingly inside and a pool of heat rested between her legs. He got up, rested a kiss on her forehead and took both plates to the kitchen. She let out a sigh of resignation. Oh, the things that man did to her.

Chapter 11

The next two days were filled with her finalizing her book and sending it to Roxanne while practicing back and forth with Holly on the escape route they had agreed upon. At first, she resisted the idea, not thinking it would be a good thing to teach her daughter but after the first test run Annette realized her fears had nothing to do with Holly at all. Her daughter seemed to feel better about them playing their "game" with her because she understood it was to help her keep safe. Annette understood her fears stemmed from having to deal with the problems they faced and it chilled her all the way through.

All this prep meant she would be staying and fighting instead of what she had been doing for so long and that was run. Annette knew this "game" could potentially help them both if it was implemented. She watched the front door swinging back and forth so many times it was like a rhythm. Her daughter excited every time she accomplished her task. They had also practiced going through the root cellar for an alternative escape.

Austin had told her to come up with a safe word, one that she could say in a bad situation that would not alarm Terry or make him suspect anything. The word she had chosen wasn't a word but a phrase. One she knew not only would she be able to use around the man but one that would give her daughter some time before he noticed. "Holly go get a beer." Terry would never suspect she was secretly telling Holly to run because Terry couldn't resist a drink. He would not have any alarm bells over Holly leaving the room to grab his beverage of choice. It almost seemed too perfect and Austin applauded her choice as well.

Trying to talk to Austin about their interesting relationship, or whatever you wanted to call this attraction between them, was like pulling teeth. She would broach the subject and he would sidestep her question or just ignore it altogether. And it was starting to get on Annette's nerves. She had done nothing wrong - they had done nothing wrong and even with Carolynn's advice swarming around in her head to wait it out she was losing patience.

Holly came bounding in from the front door, ready to go again. Her yellow sundress and pigtails bobbing behind her made Annette sigh. She loved that little girl more than her own existence. She honestly could not say where she would be if it wasn't for her daughter. Breathing heavily from running, Holly caught her mother's sleeve and yanked wildly. "Mommy can I go again! Please!"

"I don't know." Even though she was smiling at her daughter, Holly thought she was serious about her answer and showed it by dipping her chin. "Oh, okay baby." Holly's chin jumped up and her eyes were bright again. "Stay here." Annette left her in the sunroom and walked to the Livingroom. The root cellar was off the sunroom. They made sure to practice going out in different ways, the point is never to be caught, seen or heard. By now she could be in any room and say the magic words and Holly knew just what to do. Pride rippled through Annette at seeing how fast her daughter learned things.

Holly's goal was to run next door to the main house, as fast as she could and find someone. At first, it was Austin who was waiting for her but now it was

Carolynn who was waiting inside. Austin had chores to do around the ranch and wasn't available right now for practice time.

Holly made like she was talking to someone, faking a conversation was simple, and as soon as she said "Holly, can you go get me a beer?" she heard a tiny creek of the root cellar door and then silence. She smiled to herself. Her daughter was one smart cookie. Carolynn phoned over a few seconds later informing her that Holly was taking a break for lunch. Annette decided she would take one as well.

Upon opening the fridge, she realized she needed to go to the store, remembering she had already gone through the last can of soup the night before when she needed a snack since she couldn't sleep. Thank goodness for Carolynn. The woman fed them better than they had been in a long while and it started to show on her. Austin had made it clear that he wanted to see her eating or else he was going to start hand feeding her. He also noted he would have no problem feeding her as he looked at her lips. Desire plain in his eyes.

Annette shook off the memory. Right now, was not the time to get sexually excited. The only way she was going to the store though was if she got a ride since she was still out of a car. After the police took her car for evidence she decided they could just keep it. The auto shop had told her that the wires going to the engine, along with the oil line had been damaged. The total to fix it didn't seem worth it. It was time to let it go and the police station could use the donation for parts or whatever else they decided to sell it for.

Taking the opportunity to see Austin again she walked down to the barn and waited for him to get back from riding. He always liked to come in for lunch. She went around petting the horses in the corral, all four of them. Only a few minutes passed before she heard the familiar sound of hooves against the ground.

****

The sun glaring down almost blinding him, sweat dripping dust into his eyes. His hair soaked under his Stenson almost irritating his neck and his muscles ached all over. All he wanted was food, a nice hot bath, and a warm bed. He really craved a nice warm body with him in that warm bed, a specific body but he tried pushing that to the back of his mind. Getting an erection right now would not help in the least. His jeans were already sticking to him from the sweat and the thought of dealing with them getting even tighter was not appealing.

His day had been rough enough and it was only going to get more challenging by the end of it. There was too much work to be done. While he had been out rounding up a stray calf this morning one of the ranch hands from the neighboring ranch to his east came over. He had come to let him know his boss wanted him to ask if he could come over a bit earlier to see him than originally planned. He wanted to go over somethings with him. Austin said he would stop by when he got a moment away. The man had nodded and ridden off in the direction he came from. Austin had never seen the man before which wasn't so out of place. Many men found jobs on ranches for one reason or another and could leave just as easily. The odd thing was the man always kept his hat low over his eyes so he couldn't see his face and he never introduced himself. He would ask about that when he went over.

He breathed in the air when Solitaire stopped outside the barn and that is when he smelled her. A mixture of lilac and honeysuckles. It was the sweetest smell and it made his mouth water. He grew uncomfortable though as his pants got tighter. He couldn't make out her full figure, only seeing an outline. An appealing silhouette against the afternoon sun. His hands began to itch at the need to touch her. Remembering he didn't want to rush things in case she got an itch to flee helped him fight his urges to go to her and wrapped her in his arms. His past relationships had fallen apart from rushing into things and lifestyles clashing. He'd be damned if he would make that mistake again.

So instead of jumping down and pulling her to him he just took his horse into its stall and began unsaddling it. He felt her moving closer to the stall after he had put the feed into a bucket. He saw her movement as he began to brush the sweat from his horse. The sound of the horse munching away while he stroked him was soothing to him. He always loved the smells and sounds of the barn. She tapped her knuckles against the stall door when she finally made it there. "So, I was wondering if you wouldn't mind taking me into town? I want to get some things at the local store."

He arched an eyebrow at her, not break his fluid brushing movements. "I don't think I have time too. I still have to fix a fence on the east side and I got asked to go over to the Wilkin's ranch, Hugh needs something." He heard her let out a breath she must have been holding. "I also got a call this morning.

They found that missing horse." He finished combing the last of the sweat off Solitaire and walked out of the stall. He hauled the door shut and went to latch it. "Besides, I am starving. Can this wait till tomorrow?"

Annette said nothing but followed him over to the tack room as he was putting his things away. Her mind reeling from questions that she unknowingly ignored his question. "They found the horse?" Curiosity was so lovely on her that it made him break out in a grin. She was so close to him that he found himself breathing harder. Her scent swirling around him and making him a bit light-headed. He was pulled back to the present when he guessed she thought he wasn't paying attention to her. She tapped her foot on the cement floor noting she was waiting.

His shoulders slumped a bit when he turned to face her. He knew she wasn't going to like the answer to her prodding question. He knew he felt tired but he must have looked worse than he felt because she gave him a sorrowful look. He didn't like that look in her eyes. He brushed a piece of hair behind her ear as he stepped closer, looking down into her beautiful green eyes. "Yes, they found it. I offered to go help dig a hole with my excavator to bury it. Hugh said it looked like it was mauled by another animal. He thought it might have been a bear."

Surprise flickered across her features before worry took root. He wished he could read her thoughts at that moment. His hand went to cup her cheek and his thumb stroked it. His eyes locking on her mouth. They looked so kissable to him as her breath caught. Warmth radiated down his arm as she turned her head into his palm, whispering so softly he had to strain to hear it, "did they find him?"

He knew the answer she expected to hear. He shook his head hating to confirm it for her. "They didn't find a body." She turned her gaze to meet his and he dropped his hand at his side. "All they found was the horse, some torn clothing and some drag marks on the ground. They are wondering if the drag marks are from the horse or that he may have been taken by whatever go the horse." She gasped. He took another step closer to her. His need to cradle her in his arms almost overbearing. He knew he had a fifty-fifty chance of her accepting it or pushing him away. He stopped a few inches short of her fisting his hands at his sides. "That is why I need to go over there. I can only guess what else he needs to talk about."

She didn't move from her spot or saying anything to him. He found himself pulling her to him anyway. Willing to take his chances and ignoring his better instincts telling him he should stay away. She felt so good against him. Her arms wrapped under his, clinging to his shoulders as she pressed firmly against him. It felt so normal to have her held in his arms and feeling the warmth of her body against his. He rested his cheek against the top of her head. She mumbled something into his shoulder and nuzzled closer. "What was that?"

She moved to turn her head to peer up at him. "I needed this." She stated. "I've been so lonely." She pulled back more so he could see her whole face. Her eyes were sparkling pools of emerald. The most beautiful eyes he had ever seen. "By now I know you probably don't think of me or want me that way and that's fine, but I have still missed you."

Where had that come from? She thought he didn't want her! If only she knew how much he did want her. An ache shot through him at her words. He could see he had caused her pain and that was the opposite of what he was trying to do. He wanted to protect her, he was supposed to be protecting her and he failed. What's worse is he had been lonely too. Miserably so. He has been doing nothing but thinking about touching her, holding her, and so much more. Rolling over in bed to cold emptiness was awful. It caused him to be restless at night which in turn made him more tired. He even missed hearing that little munchkin of hers yapping in her room at night till she passed out.

She turned to leave but he pulled her back, lifting her chin to look at him. He noted the lack of fight left in her at that moment and frowned. "Let's get one thing straight right now", he barked. "I do want you. So much so that I have been depriving myself thinking I was in return saving you heartache."

She reeled back like she had been struck and she tried pulling away again. He held tightly to her upper arms not letting her get away, her voice came out high pitched, "Heartache? From what?" The look she gave him, a mix between "how dare you" and "I need you" made him hold his breath. He flexed his arm muscles and released his hold on her. It was the only thing he could do to let out his frustration. He needed to get ahold of himself before he went stir crazy and took her right here in the barn. Those eyes looking at him like that, pleading to him with fire had his insides heating up.

He rubbed some of the tension out of his neck before answering. "From me. I'm not the best at relationships darling. I like you a whole hell of a lot. And instead of messing things up with you I have been trying to make space. I know you have had it hard too." His eyes dropped to the ground. He would have looked anywhere but at her face right then. Knowing he wears his heart on his sleeve.

She sounded so small at that moment. "Wait. What?" She sounded unsure and he knew he had done that. "I didn't even think you liked me like that anymore." She pinched the bridge of her nose and closed her eyes. "What are you saying exactly?"

He blew out a breath, watching her. "Whatever this attraction is between us, I truth, scares the crap outta me. I don't trust it. I am not used to feeling this strongly about someone this fast. I don't want to start something just to end up with nothing. So, I thought it was best if we cooled it down." She dropped her hand and placed it flat against his chest, putting space between them.

She looked up at him half smiling. Oh, how he loved that smile. Just remember the feeling of her mouth had him getting tingles spreading through him. "You have strong feelings for me?" She followed his eyes when he dropped them. This time it was her who nudged his chin up.

"Yes." Was all he could get out as he stared at her. Her eyes blinking back tears. He placed his hand over hers that was still resting on his chest.

Her smile reached both corners now making her face light up. "Good. I feel the same way about you."

Nothing else needed to be said. He heard exactly what he needed to. Wrapping his arms around her hips he lifted her up and pressed her chest into his. He held her there as he claimed her mouth. Both letting out little groans at the ecstasy the felt. The kiss getting more intense. Both her hands sliding up his chest and holding onto his shoulders as she opened her mouth to his prodding tongue. He loved the taste of her. Sweet and salty. It made him grow even more ridged reminding him he was in a state of dirty disarray but didn't care. He had her here, against him and she was opening to him. She held onto him tighter, sliding her hands under his arms to grip his shoulders from behind. He moved one hand to rest at the back of her neck and the other cupping her bottom. *God, she was heaven.* He was so turned on.

He backed her up against the wall of the tack room. Growling against her lips as one of her hands slid down from his shoulder, over his stomach, to cradle him through his jeans. She slowly rubbed him when he grabbed her ass tighter. He forgot how to breathe. He heard her moan against his lips one instant and then next she wrapped her leg around his.

He moaned into her mouth just as Solitaire kicked over the feed bucket and slamming his hoof into the wall, scaring them both. They jumped breaking the kiss. Austin instinctively placed both hands on the wall above her head shielding her and pinning her to the wall. He wasn't sure what it was at first but when the realization hit he backed up breaking contact. Annette was giggling under him.

"Dang animal." He ground out. Frustration in his tone. "What's so funny?"

She took a breath from the giggling and moved out from under his arms. He stood up straight then. Missing the feel of her already. "I think he is telling us to get a room." That had both of them laughing. He looked at her. Her hair was a little mused but her dress looked like she had been rolling around in the dirt from her pressing against him. "Alright old McDonald, are you ready for lunch?" she said as she shook out her hair and brushed her hands down her dress. Ineffectively getting the dirt off.

She ran her eyes the length of him, lingering on his crotch before meeting his eyes again. He saw her tongue darting out and wet her lips in a teasing gesture. It had him standing straighter and his nostrils flared. "because I am starving." She suddenly turned away and headed back out the barn. He adjusted his pants and calmed his breathing before following her out. He was starving too for more than one type of food. She was going to drive him insane one way or the other and he had a feeling it was going to be one exciting ride.

Chapter 12

Holly came running up to Annette when she walked into the house. She was sprinkled head to toe with white powder and licking something off of a spoon. She pulled it out of her mouth with a big pop sound before clinging to her mother's leg with one arm and pulling her toward the kitchen with the other. "Mommy! Mommy! We made cooks! We made cooks!" the little girl said. "You made what?" was her reply but her daughter didn't say anything else until they got to the kitchen. Carolynn was in an apron and putting a baking pan in the oven full of cookies. *Oh, now I know*, she thought, smiling to herself.

Holly put the spoon back in her mouth and clung to her leg with both arms now, hugging her. Carolynn straightened and turned to them. Her hair wasn't a strand out of place but her apron with all the cows printed on it looked like it had been through warfare. Other than the straps around her neck, every square inch was covered in flour. "Phew," she said as she wiped her hands on her apron. No way she could get her hands clean on it with how covered it was. Annette heard the banging of boots on the porch and a few seconds later the front porch creaked open and shut. Annette felt the heat rising up her neck and pooling in her cheeks. Carolynn rubbed her hands together and gave an all too knowing smirk off her lips. "You better go clean up before you eat! I am not having dirt and mud all on my floor!" She yelled to Austin from the kitchen, still staring at Annette.

A mumble of noises and a grunt was all they heard before stomping up the stairs followed. All the girls in the kitchen let out a small giggle. Holly let go of her and walked to the sink to put the spoon in. She turned to go but Carolynn chimed in, "Where are you going little lady? We need to wash our hands and get ready for lunch." The woman pulled a stool over to the sink for her daughter to climb on. Holly climbed up and stood to wait. "Now do you remember our song for washing hands?" That got Annette's attention. She moved to sit on a stool at the island and watched the two washing their hands. Holly gave a nod and waited for the water to come on before starting to sing with Carolynn. "Row, row, row your boat. Gently down the stream. Merrily, merrily, merrily. Now, our hands are clean." She watched in awe as the two did it again, this time Holly was the only one singing. She let out a sigh just before they finished and two hands laid on her shoulders making her jump in her seat at the unexpected contact. "Shhhh," he whispered in her ear. She could feel the smile in his voice, sending delicious chills down her spine. He kissed the top of her head and squeezed her shoulders before he let go. He sat in the chair next to her just as they finished drying their hands. Holly let out a squeal of excitement when she turned around and saw Austin standing there.

Holly ran right over to him and put her arms up to be picked up. He obliged and scooped her up. She wrapped her arms around his neck and squeezed. "You're here," is the muffled statement she said into his neck. He smiled and laughed when he squeezed her back. "Where else would I be sweet pea," he retorted before pulling her back and looking at her. "And it seems just after the dust bowl hit. What did you do in here?" Holly yelled out, "Made Cooks!" Then she busted out laughing and squealing when he started tickling her. "You made cookies? You are so talented." The whole time tickling her. Their laughter made the other two women laugh as well. When Holly couldn't stand it anymore he relented in his tickling.

Annette stared at the two of them and something washed through her at the sight. She could not shake the notion that she was falling in love with this man. *Is this what it feels like to be happy*, she questioned herself. So many more thoughts slammed into her. Can we really make it work here? What if Terry finds them, then what? Can she ever see herself leaving this place, these people, this man? Just the thought of leaving him brought a sick feeling to her stomach she didn't want to dwell on. The happy moments, like this one, where what life was about, weren't they? The joy on her daughter's face and the way they both connected made her heart sing to life. We will try and make this work, she finalized in her mind. I now have something else to fight for. A happy family.

The clucking of Carolynn's tongue brought her mind back to the present. She turned to look at the other woman who was leaning against the kitchen counter staring at her. A blush crept up her neck and she looked away. Holly squirmed down off Austin lap and was pulling him into the Livingroom. Babbling something about drawings she must have made. The smile on his face and a small shrug before he let her lead him away. "Five minutes till lunch you two," Carolyn hollered after them. The woman motioned for Annette to get the plates out before strolling over to the fridge and pulling out some containers. They started piling each plate with food before Carolynn spoke. "So where did you go just now?"

Not sure what the woman was referring to she looked at her questioningly and confusion must have been on her face because the other woman replied, "you were staring off into space a moment ago." The whole time not looking straight at her, just piling up more food on each plate.

"I was just lost in thought I guess. Been a crazy couple of days." She wasn't sure how much the woman picked up on and she wasn't going to get into it right now when she wasn't sure of everything herself. "More like a crazy couple of weeks, months, and years I reckon from all the things you and that sweet child have been through." The other woman replied with another cluck of her tongue.

All Annette could do was agree, "Yea. It can only go up from, here right?" She felt herself asking more than stating. She had not once felt unwelcome in their home and yet right at that moment, she needed verification from someone, anyone that life would eventually be more than just running. The elderly lady stopped what she was doing and turned to her.

Annette just stared at the plate in front of her. "That is right. It will get better. Hasn't it already?" Carolynn placed her hands on her hips, "and now you do not have to do it alone. You have us child and you are not going anywhere." Carolynn placed her finger under her chin to force her to look up at her. The other woman's eyes were so full of hope that it surprised Annette. "When you start believing in it, it will start to feel real too." Annette couldn't help it, tears began streaming down her cheeks. Unbidden tears she couldn't hold back anymore. "Shhh child," Carolynn cooed as she brought her into a hug. "Let it out. It's ok to cry sometimes. It shows you that things are changing and you are strong enough to handle it." Shaking and sniffling with the tears, she let the other woman hold her. Allowed the comforting words to wash over her. "Just like they say, the Lord never gives us more than we can handle. If this is your burden it is to teach you something or to lead you somewhere. I firmly believe He lead you to us. You can lean on us anytime. We already consider you family."

Annette pulled back to look up at the other woman. Sniffles breaking the silence for a moment as she saw the sincerity in the other woman's gaze. *She is right*, she thought. They will get through this, and they will overcome it. The sound of footsteps and chatter coming back into the room had Carolynn taking plates to the island. This gave Annette time to wipe at her tear-streaked face and blow out a breath. She just hoped she didn't look awful when she turned around to join them a moment later.

****

The sun had cooled down some when Austin finally made it back out to the barn to check on his horse. He decided to take his truck over to the Wilkin's ranch to talk to Hugh instead of riding Solitaire back out in this heat. It may have cooled down some but he didn't want the horse to get too burned out. The whole time he was checking on the horse and driving was a daze. He couldn't stop thinking about how Anette had looked when he came back into the kitchen. He could tell she had been crying. Her cheeks were streaked from tears and her eyes were puffy. She sniffled a few times in between eating and talking to Holly.

She looked at him a few times, but not for long. He wanted to know what could have happened in the short time they had been in the Livingroom. He wasn't going to ask her in front of everyone, he knew better than that, but he was worried. What if something bad had happened? What If she decided she was going to leave and didn't know how to tell him? That brought pain and with it anger to his chest. He slammed his hand on the steering wheel. No! If she wanted to leave she better talk to him first. He would talk her out of it. He would plead, beg, or grovel if he had to. She was not going anywhere. He knew she felt the attraction between them, she had said as much. He knew he was in love with her. He might not understand it but he loved them both and was not going to let them just walk away. He couldn't.

His short trip next door was filled with so many questions running through his head. Questions he wouldn't have answers to until he got a chance to sit down and have a conversation with Annette. For now, though they would have to wait.

He pulled up to the beige brick ranch house with its massive porch and stopped his truck. As soon as he did Hugh had come walking out onto the porch and down the front steps. The medium build man had a salt and pepper beard matching his short-trimmed hair. To Austin, he still had a hard-handed presence about him but now he knew the man also had a kind heart. His step was a little slower and favored his right leg a little more than the last time he saw him. He held out a hand in greeting. Austin took it and greeted him before following him to the barn. "How has the ranch been? How is Carolann doing?" Hugh was the only man around who had ever used his Grandmas's real name, other than his Grandpa. Probably since they knew each other all their lives.

"She is doing good. The ranch has its ups and downs. Our heard has been steady. I am thinking about adding another dozen or so next year depending on how many calves we have this year." He followed Hugh to four horses that were already saddled and waiting in the barn.

One ranch hand and Hughs foreman, Cliff, whom Austin had known for over two decades were waiting for them. Their conversation stopped when they approached. "Hey Austin," Cliff said. Austin gave him a nod. The other man just looked at him and smiled.

"So," Austin said in general, "What exactly are we going to do? I thought I was helping you haul in and bury the horse." Hugh cleared his throat, "You are. We already dug the hole yesterday but before we move it I wanted you to see the area to see if anything looks off. I know you were worried about that gal staying at your place." Hugh shook of a hat he had on a hook and placed it on his head.

"Didn't you already check the scene? I thought the Sherriff and his deputy already came out there." Austin looked back and forth between the men.

"Oh, he was out here. They took some pictures and walked around but they didn't find anything. I thought you might want a shot before move it all." Austin just nodded his head. The other man was right. He would like a chance to look around before they removed everything. At the very least he could give Annette some peace of mind if it was nothing.

"Alright, let's mount up so we can get this done. My knee isn't going to get any better standing around." Austin looked at the man, focusing on his knee a bit too long. "The docs say my arthritis is getting bad and the years I spent on the rodeo are finally catching up to me. What else you gonna do?" He shrugged it off and went climbing on one of the mounts. Austin followed, along with the two other men.

He made a mental note to have Carolynn send him over something to eat and stop by for a visit. The man's wife had passed four years ago and he could only imagine how lonely he must be from missing her. Having some home cooking and some company might help perk up his spirits. After a good ten minutes in silence, Austin figured they could pass the time talking about some other matters.

"So, Hugh, you still looking for someone to breed your Arabian mare?"

Still looking ahead, he replied, "I haven't found anyone who wants to do it unless it is with a mustang and that is not what I am looking for." The man let out a gruff noise and wiped at his forehead. "If you're still looking I would let Solitaire take a crack at her if you want."

At that statement, Hugh stopped focusing on the landscape and turned his head. He snapped it over so fast he thought the other man might have whiplash. With narrowed eyes, "Why? I thought you told Jamenson you would never breed that horse unless it was worth your wild and he offered you a shit ton of money, and you still turned him down. I don't have that kind of capital to put into something like that."

Austin gave him a smile and casually said, "Jameson is an asshat that I wouldn't let clean my boots. That man is always looking to exploit anything he can." The other man relaxed and turned to look back at the landscape. "Besides, you are next to kin for me. If you need help you can always let me know."

The other two men stayed behind them a few feet staying silent the whole time. Hugh didn't utter a word for so long that Austin wasn't sure if he had heard him or not. He was just about to say something again when he finally spoke. "What would you want to breed him?"

Austin grinned to himself. He knew the other man couldn't resist. "We can work something out when we get back." The other man just nodded saying nothing else. Almost a half-hour went by before they reached the spot. It was on the far side of the spread where they farm corn. The stalks were so high you couldn't see anything unless you had been looking for it. The end of the crop butted up against a decent size hill. They all demounted and walked over to the spot. The horse was laying partially up the hill and was ripped open. Blood trailed down the hill and on the other side, it looked to be a spot for a fire pit. There were clothes thrown about everywhere and ripped into pieces. Some were in the fire, charred and there were marks in the dirt. Austin did notice that there were also a bunch of boot prints everywhere too but not sure if they were from who was here or from the men checking the spot out. One thing he didn't see was any sign a bear or large cat had been here.

"How did you guys know this was here? I am standing here and I still can't see over all the corn." Cliff spoke up, "Leim here, "pointing to the guy next to him, "was riding fences and heard some noises over here. He came over and found this." The man looked right at Austin nodding his head. Leim spoke up next, "I put out the fire when I got here in case a fire broke out and then ran to tell Cliff."

Austin couldn't sense the man was lying. So, he shrugged it off. "I do not see any sign that another animal was here or did this. No droppings, no claw marks, no prints, nothing. The marks on the horse look more like a blade than an animal." Hugh was bobbing his head up and down in agreement. "That is exactly what I thought," he said.

It took all the men two hours to bury the horse and clean up the area enough to be satisfied. They were sweaty, even though it had cooled down to a bearable amount. The sun was setting and the men were officially tired and ready to finish up their chores for the day. After returning to the barn they all dismounted and two men tended to the horses while Hugh and Austin headed back out towards his truck. "So, what did you need me to come here early for if that was all that needed to be done?"

Hugh looked confused for a moment. "I didn't need you to come here early. I thought you were excited to get started when I saw you driving up to the house a whole hour early." Austin looked even more befuddled than the other man.

"The horses were already saddled when I got here." He replied. Looking towards the barn then back at the man. "They were already saddled earlier when the men used them to check fences. When you got here there was no point in unsaddling them just to redo it. We just took them."

"But you sent one of your ranch hands early this morning to tell me to meet you earlier because you needed to talk to me about some things."

Hugh's eyes got narrowed. He scowled at Austin, "What man? I didn't send any man. All my hands are accounted for that I know of."

Chapter 13

Annette brought Holly back to the cottage after lunch. Her skin was still humming from the contact with Austin in the barn earlier. She was so happy to know that he had feelings for her that the entire time she had been home she was humming to herself. A melody that was stuck in her head. Holly started doing it with her too. Annette had placed Holly in the tub with lots of bubbles just the way she liked it after she herself got a quick shower to clean off all the dust she received from Austin. Leaving her daughter to giggle and play with her favorite bath toys, she went downstairs to put her dress in the wash.

She was starting the machine when a knock started at the door and she went to go see who it was. She opened the main door leaving the screen door in place. A man stood there with sunglasses, a cowboy hat, and a bandanna covering the lower part of his face. She thought it was weird, but the wind did pick up and with all the dust she kind of understood the bandanna. A lot of working men used them when they didn't want the dust and dirt to get into their mouth or nose. He held a vase with a bouquet with a mixture of daisies, lily of the valley flowers and wildflowers.

She smiled brightly and opened the screen door. "Can I help you?" She took in his jeans and a wrinkly blue plaid shirt. Kind of an odd uniform for a delivery man but maybe they were more casual out here. "I have a delivery for Mrs. O'leary," if she had been paying attention to his tone she may have noticed his sneer when he said his last name but she was too focused on the gift and getting back to her daughter.

She replied with a "Thank you," as she took the vase from him, only slightly noticing the tightened grip he had on it before letting it go. She closed the screen door and waited for him to step off the porch before closing the main door and clicking the lock, something she noted, she never felt the need to do before. *Odd*, she thought. After placing the vase down on the kitchen table she brushed the sensation off that something was not quite right. She grabbed the card on it and smiled to herself when she read:

I'll be seeing you soon. Can't wait to touch you.

She could only guess the flowers had been from Austin. Such a sweet gesture. She was still smiling when she went upstairs to wash and dry her daughter. After getting her dressed in floral pajamas they both sat down to read a book on the couch.

After asking to read the same story for the third time, a story about an elephant who becomes friends with a mouse, her precious daughter yawns and says, "Mommy, I hungry." Annette looks down at her and smiles. Rubbing her arm, she eases up to look at the clock on the end table. "Where has the time gone?" It had only been noon when she got home but now it was easing on four-thirty. "You completely missed nap time too. Oh well."

Sitting up Holly stretched next to her. "Can we eat?" She asked softly turning her head to look up at her. At that moment Annette's stomach did a loud grumble too. Holly started giggling and that made her laugh too. After a few fits of laughter, the phone rang. Annette got up to go grab the phone from its place on the wall, an older yellow phone with a cord attached, and said "Hello."

Carolynn's voice came out all rushed and breathless. "One second Deary," A clanging of dishes came from the background. "I had to pull out some biscuits from the oven." She was catching her breath for a minute, which made her smile on the phone. Holly called her from the other room. Annette leaned over the wall with the cord trailing to press her fingers to her lips to motion for her to be quiet. Then she leaned back. "Is there something you need Carolynn?" Annette asked, still smiling.

"Yes, Dear. I am calling to tell you dinner will be ready in twenty minutes I wanted to ask you to bring over some salt if you have it. Seems I ran out and forgot to grab some more." Annette agreed and told her they would be over shortly before hanging up.

Upon entering the Livingroom Holly ran up to her clinging to her leg. "Mommy. Mommy. I saw a man walking out with the horses." Her daughter seemed excited. Annette went to look out the window. She saw a small cluster of horses in the closest pasture and the farther one had cows dotting the landscape. She never saw a man but assumed it could have been one of the men who came to help Austin with the herd or maybe her daughter seeing things. "Ok munchkin. We are going to Carolynn's for dinner. Go potty while I grab what she needs. Be quick I don't want to take too long." Holly dashed away running up the stairs.

****

Driving like the Devil was on his heels he sped down the driveway. He probably broke all the speed limits he could think of to make it back home. Hugh and Cliff in the truck following him after they realized that the other man didn't send anyone to fetch him earlier in the day. His heart pounding in his chest at the thought of Terry coming near his family, that included Annette and Holly. He cursed himself for not charging his phone enough. He hadn't realized it had died until he got in the truck and was already driving.

The sun was almost gone as he saw the outline of his house come into view. He reached it gravel remnants from the paving crew Annette had hired flying around in his rushed stop. He barreled out of his truck and up the steps just as Hugh and cliff climbed out of their truck with shotguns, right on his heel. Slamming through the front door not even worried about dragging in mud and dirt, he yelled out, "Gran! Annette! Where are all of you?!"

He saw the women jump up just as he strode into the Livingroom. Surprise, shock and concern on their faces. "What in the blazes got up your backside young man?! Scaring the living daylights out of the whole county with that racket?" Carolynn placing a hand on her chest.

Annette looked right at him and moved past the other woman, stopping only inches from him. "Austin? What's wrong? Did something happen?"

Before he could answer the other men barreled into the house and crowed into the living room, shotguns in hand. "Everyone ok? Anyone hurt?" Cliff rushed out as he scanned the room. Hugh letting out a sigh and walking around the room.

Carolynn narrowed her eyes at all the men when Hugh finished his turn about the room. Annette hadn't moved at all, both of them staring at each other the whole time. Austin's heart calmed down a bit at the sight of her, knowing she was ok and nothing had happened in his absence.

"Hugh Wilkins, if you and your man do not put those guns away I will tear your hides!" Carolynn snapped, placing her hands on her hips. "And you," she pointed to Austin, "Better tell me what is going on and why you all are ruining my clean floor with this outburst!"

Anette gave a slight quirk of her lips in a small smile before he tore his eyes away to look at his Gran. "Sorry Gran but I believe Terry might have been here or had someone working with him and needed to make sure you all were ok." At the mention of the name, he felt Annette flinch slightly. "I was out doing rounds earlier and remember I mentioned at lunch I was asked to go over earlier than planned?" Carolynn and Annette both nodded.

Hugh chimed in then. "I didn't send no man. All my men were accounted for on the ranch." Carolynn frowned at that. So, Austin decided to clarify, "It had to be Terry or someone with him trying to get me away from the ranch. Not that I am not grateful for my ladies to be fine, but I do not understand why if he didn't plan to do anything?" Anette looked like she was going to throw up and that made him furious. He wanted to ease her pain and this other person kept reminding her of it. If only he could remove it completely.

He scanned the room again and realized Holly wasn't there. "Where is munchkin?" He said a little too loudly. Carolynn had put her hands down now and came closer. "Poor thing got tuckered out after dinner and we put her in bed upstairs."

"I'll go check on her. Hugh. Cliff." He turned his head to the men behind him, "Can you go check the rest of the house while I sweep upstairs?" Both men nodded and left the room. Austin pulled Annette into his arms and held her. Her warmth reassuring to him. She wrapped her arms around him and resting on the back of his shoulders. "We are all right," she said in assurance but he didn't miss the small shiver run through her.

He kissed her so lightly on the lips he still felt the air between them and then he left the room and charged upstairs. A scan of the hallway and the rooms upstairs came up empty. He found Holly still asleep in bed. He went over to her, in her floral pajamas and brushed the hair out of her face. Smiling as she let out a small noise and snuggled further under the covers. He kissed her head before scanning her room and softly leaving the room, only partially closing the door. He crept back downstairs to meet the other men in the dining room. The women joined them when sirens started in the distance. Carolynn wrapping one arm around Annette.

"I called Sherriff Townsend on our way here to let him know something was going on. That's prolyl him now," Hugh chimed in. Austin noted how the elderly man stood up a bit straighter when Carolynn was in the room. The two women visibly relaxed some.

Cliff already on his way out the front door towards the arriving police car, the rest of them following. Sherriff Townsend slammed on his breaks, hand going to his pistol as he climbed out of the patrol car. "What's going on?" He demanded.

Cliff being the first one out stated, "Nothing yet. We scanned the house and nothing is out of the ordinary." Sherriff Townsend took in the surroundings of outside before he took his hand off his pistol.

Austin still on the porch waved for them all to go inside.

****

Annette and Carolynn came out of the kitchen to the dining room with tea, coffee and a tray of sandwiches after the men had all taken a seat. Hugh stared at Carolynn a bit too long as she moved around the room and Annette notice the other woman seemed oblivious. The men said their thanks before discussing what had happened to warrant calling Tony down here. Annette listened from her seat, not saying a thing. She got the gist of everything, but she was still confused about what Terry must have been planning if nothing happened in the hours Austin was gone.

Hugh and Tony must have been thinking the same thing because they mentioned that it made no sense. Cliff scratched his head for a minute before saying, "maybe this was only meant to keep you off-kilter? Make you on edge?" The men all began to nod except Austin. He sat there staring into his cup. All the men's eyes rested on him for a few stretched out moments before he spoke. "I am not sure he even meant for me to find out." Austin rubbed the back of his neck, "and if that is the case then he was planning something. I am not sure what just yet."

He looked at her then. A hard stare that spoke volumes. He was worried, for her, for all of them. She saw the clenching of his jaw, marveled in the way it made her tummy do flip flops. He was so strong and determined and it made her warm all over. She knew now wasn't the time for it but she couldn't help herself. Still staring at her he said, "we need to do a thorough check of the lands tomorrow. It's too dark now. Make sure no one has been squatting or doing anything else." She instantly missed the intensity of his gaze when he broke it to look at the men. Each one nodding and murmuring in agreement.

Carolynn who had been silent this whole time started clucking her tongue. Something obviously on her mind but she still kept silent. She got up to start clearing the table, Hugh jumping up to help her. Cliff and Tony were in conversation which gave some time for Annette to talk to Austin across the table. She waited for him to look at her again and when he did she all but melted. His smile mirrored her own. She placed her hand over the table to squeeze his. "Thank you for the flowers today. It was very sweet." Something shifted in his eyes. He looked confused as if he didn't know what she was talking about. He confirmed her suspicion with the next sentence out of his mouth.

"What flowers?" She frowned. Thinking about the card and wondering if he was serious. But why would he be joking? And if he didn't send them, then who did? "I got a delivery of flowers with a card. That wasn't from you?" She tilted her head to the side. Tony and Cliff looking at them, probably noticing something was going on. Austin let go of her hand and stood just as a smiling Carolynn and Hugh came back into the room. Their smiles erased when they saw Austin.

Tension rising in the room, so thick she almost felt the crackle. His voice was so low and tinged with something fierce when he spoke, "I never sent any flowers. Where are they now?" Annette swallowed very audibly before telling him. He looked at the men who also nodded agreement to something. What that was she had no idea. He looked back at her. "What did the card say?" She told him and his eyes seemed to get a darker shade of grey and not in a good way.

Everyone in the dining room jumped when they heard a *thunk, thunk, thunk* coming down the stairs. A still sleepy Holly came in the room with a blanket dragging behind her and she was rubbing her eyes. "Mommy?" Annette rushed over to her and everyone let the breath they had been holding go. She picked her up and held her close. "Did you have a nice nap baby?" Loving the feeling of her daughter in her arms and having her press her head to her shoulder was so comforting. No matter what happened, this little girl was everything. Austin came up behind her rubbing her back with one hand and Holly's mess of hair with the other. He murmured in her ear, "my two beautiful girls." Then he kissed hers and Holly's head.

She turned to look at him, smiling. No words needed at that moment. She felt pure joy at his words and didn't want to ruin it. "You and Gran stay here while we go check out the cottage. We will be right back. Hugh will stay here too in case anyone comes while we are gone." She nodded her head in agreement, Holly still laying on her shoulder. Her daughter's soft breathing in her ear.

When all the men walked out Carolynn motioned for Annette to go sit on the couch with Holly till she woke up some. As she sat there, her daughter snuggled up on her, everything came crashing down on her conscious. She brought this on everyone. Her problems with her ex could have been harmful to those around her and that is exactly what she didn't want. A breeze blew in from the cracked window and lightly swept her hair from her neck. The sun had gone down an hour before and outside was lit only by moonlight.

When she thought about leaving, she got a burning, stinging pain in her chest. She knew she could never leave Austin or Carolynn. Not now. This place had felt comforting from the beginning but now it was home. She knew it in her soul. Austin had already told her she was staying; an order more than a request and that memory brought a quirk to her lips. Carolynn was wiping her hands on her apron when she walked back into the living room with Hugh on her tail. She had noticed the other man had been either interested in her or very concerned, or both since he had arrived. Annette thought it was very sweet.

I hope this all ends soon," she said to Hugh when she entered the room. The other man nodded in agreement. "Do you need anything Dearie?" She asked Annette. "No. I am just waiting like everyone else." Unsatisfied with the reply Carolynn chimed in, "I'll go grab you a glass of tea and a juice for that one," motioning to Holly who started to stir in her arms before turning and walking back out of the room.

Holly put her hands-on Annette's chest and pushed up to look at her. "Mommy, I need to pee." Wiping a strand of hair out of her daughter's face, "Ok baby. Let's go to the potty."

Chapter 14

Annette heard muffled voices when she came out of the bathroom with Holly walking in front of her. Her daughter ran up to Austin when she found him in the living room with everyone else. He turned to her, smiled and picked her up. Holly putting her hands around his neck and squeezing. "You're late," Holly said very loudly. Everyone got quiet and looked at her. Austin just replied with, "Late for what?" Holly let out a big puff of air as if to say – *you should already know* – before responding with, "Dinner. We ate. You not here. Why you not here?" She gave such a serious pouty face that Annette stifled a laugh. Austin must have known how serious Holly was because he kept a straight face. She commended him for it.

"I am sorry munchkin. We had work to get done. Did you save me any food or did you eat it all?" At that Holly shook her head and looked at Carolynn. Carolynn gave a click of her tongue insisted, "There is still food left in the fridge." At that Holly smiled. Austin still holding Holly walked over to Annette and kissed her on the forehead. "I am so glad you all are safe. I was so worried." Before she could reply the men started talking again and drowned out the sound in the room.

"There was no one in when we checked," Cliff told Hugh. The older man scratching his beard. Carolynn sitting down in a chair next to where he stood listening intently. "But we did find the so-called flowers and note."

"Annette, can you tell us what the delivery man looked like?" Terry pinned his gaze on her. She quickly relayed what she could remember about him, how she felt a bit off at his presence. "Did anything he said seem suspicious?" Annette shook her head and just said, "no but the note I thought was from Austin seems eerie now." She shivered in his embrace.

"Are these them?" Tony asked Annette pointing to a vase on the table. It took a moment for Annette to understand he was talking to her. She didn't even notice the vase of flowers until then either. She figured she was just so stressed out that she was not paying enough attention to things. "Yes. But what does he mean so-called flowers? They look like normal flowers to me."

Austin wrapped the arm not holding up holly around her shoulders. Effectively pulling her closer to him. A chill of worry that something was wrong and excitement at his touch ran through her simultaneously. Tony shook his head at her. When he spoke, it was to the whole room. The tone of his voice very firm but with an edge to it, she hadn't heard him use before. She knew it must be from anger he was trying to hold back. "Whoever gave you these knew what they were giving you and they probably planned it out. Daisies are harmless. Lily of the Valley is a flower used to signify death." With that Annette's look of - *how in the world could you know that* - must have been plain on her face when he replied, "I dated a florist for a while." He cleared his throat and went on, "the other random flower missed in, well some of them are not flowers." That caught her attention and her eyes focused on him.

"These red berries looking things are poisonous and these leaves are poison ivy. Did you or Holly touch any of these plants?"

"No just the vase. I picked them up and placed them on the table like I told you." Annette's voice got very low. Austin turned his eyes on her. "What's wrong?"

"Terry is the only one who knows I am allergic to poison ivy." Looking at the floor instead of at him. If she had her suspicions before, she had none now. Austin gave a low grumble, tightening his grip around her shoulders.

Tony ran his finger through his hair that was already a mess from being under his uniform hat. "Holly didn't touch them either?" He questioned. "No, but why would that matter? She isn't allergic to them."

Tony let out a big rush of air and looked very serious and very mad at that moment. "Does she still have a tendency to put things in her mouth? She likes to eat berries, right?" It hit her then. The berries on the sticks were poisonous and there were tons of them in the bouquet. If Holly had tried to eat them she could have gotten very sick or even... she didn't want to finish that thought. She swayed and got very dizzy. Holly squirmed to be let down when Austin moved to hold her up.

"You ok?" He asked as he let Holly down. By then all the men and Carolynn stood and moved closer. She put a hand to brace herself on his arm. "I'm fine just a little dizzy all of a sudden."

Carolynn in the background clucking her tongue again. A sound Annette noticed soothed her a bit. "You all have scared the poor girl. Shame on y'all. Look at her she is white as my sheets. Austin, go sit her down in the living room I will go grab her some soup."

Holly rushed out of the room to the living room anyway. Annette assumed it was to watch TV since she heard the faint noise from the other room. Annette made a gasp when Austin picked her up into his arms to carry her. Her own voice sounded off to her ears, "He meant to hurt Holly too. All those berries could have killed her." She noted the nods and grim expressions of the men in the room before she was ushered out. Austin said nothing as he placed her so gently down on the couch. "But why even worry about you? I mean why bother having you leave early in the first place?" She couldn't ignore the questions in her head.

Austin knelt down beside her. His solemn expression and the look in his eyes showed so many emotions at once. She already knew he was worried for her, for all of them, and she couldn't be more grateful to have him in her life then she was at that moment. "I wouldn't be around to help if you got too sick or if Holly did. My assumption, "His voice dropped to a wisher in case Holly could hear, "is that if you two were vulnerable enough he could just come on in and do whatever his twisted mind wanted."

****

Damn it. He knew he shouldn't have told her what had been on his mind since checking the cottage. He already white skin looked to get even whiter at his words when realization set in. He silently chided himself. She needed rest and not to stress about this. He would handle it any way he could. The men in the other room all agreed on the way back to the house they would find him, and soon. Alive or not he would not keep bothering them or putting lives in danger again. "You two are going to stay here in the house until we find him." He put a hand up when she went to protest, "I know you like your space but I can't protect you and monitor things if you are out of my sight. At least here Carolynn is around too." At that, Carolynn walked into the room and spoke up, "That's a wise idea and not up for discussion."

Holly turned around at that, "We sleepover?" Carolynn beamed at her. Placing the cup of soup in Annette's hands she looked at Holly, "Yes. Sleepover for a lot of days. Isn't that fun?" Holly excitedly jumped up and down saying "yes, yes, yes." Over and over again. "Good." Carolynn let out a chuckle. "Now you can come with me and we will go and find a snack before we brush your teeth for bed." An excited Holly grabbed the other woman's hand before being lead out to the kitchen. Effectively leaving Annette and Austin alone.

"We can't stay in this house forever. I can't hide here forever. We will eventually need to do things. Besides I don't even have a change of clothes." He didn't miss how her hands shook with the cup. He just wished he could take the painful memories away and just let her be happy, here with him. Giving her a weak smile, "You can always wear one of my shirts again. It looked good on you last time." That got her attention. She looked at him and a few seconds later a pretty blush crept up into her cheeks. She gave him a smile, even if it was small and very short-lived, he took it gratefully. Trying to distract her was his main goal right now. "The other stuff we can figure out later. We have the time to discuss all that, just right now is not a great time. But be sure, when we have a moment, I will talk to you about it." She looked down at his lips then and his dick twitched in his pants. He was beginning to get a semi hard-on at just the knowledge she was thinking about kissing him.

He couldn't focus on that right now or else he wouldn't get anything done. He also thought it would be rude to keep the men in the other room waiting on him. Standing up, he brushed a kiss against her lips. She sighed against him at the feel and his heart expanded at the noise. "Now, you finish that soup and I will be back in to take ou upstairs for a change of clothes and a shower. Gran can put Holly to bed if you are unable to. She never minds it." He winked at her before walking back out, leaving a still pale Annette sipping on her cup.

After another half hour of talking to the men about his suspicions, which Tony agreed with, they came to the conclusion of having a search and hunting party rounded up tomorrow to go looking around the surrounding property. When everyone drove off down the driveway Austin stood outside a little longer. He looked up at the stars and just awe at the universe above him. He breathed it all in. Loving the land, he called home he realized he should have never left to begin with. The moon shining so brightly tonight illuminated the whole landscape. The barn to the house was very visible even at this time of night. Nights like this he felt like he should stay out and enjoy every minute of it, but the reality of having to be up in a few short hours to work the ranch and then go out with a group of men searching had him crashing back down. He turned to walk back inside.

Something moved near the barn and he turned to look. He thought it was ear the side of the round pen but when he looked closer he didn't see anything. A few more minutes of staring were fruitless and he shrugged it off and walked back inside. If it was something the horses would wake up and make noise but they didn't make a pep. *Probably a groundhog or bird,* he thought.

He got inside just as Holly was hugging her mother goodnight. She jumped over to him and put her hands up for him to pick her up. "Night -Stin" was all she said before kissing his cheek and pushing to be let back down. She ran after Carolynn up the stairs to be put into bed.

Annette was looking at him. Her empty soup cup sitting on the table next to her. He turned, shut and locked the door. After shaking off and removing his boots, placing his hat on the coat rack, and locking the back door, he came back into the living room. Smells from outside mingled with the savory of the chicken soup she had been eating. A soft glow came from the lamps on the table and she looked so small wrapped up in the plaid blanket. He went to her, helped her up from the couch to look down into her eyes. Checking her over he noted her complexion looking a bit better. She at least didn't look like she was going to faint at any second anymore.

He placed a finger under her chin to make her look up at him before he spoke. Tears rimmed her eyes and it about broke his heart. "Tonight has been very stressful. I am sorry this is happening but we will deal with this. I promise you." She went to move her face away again but he firmly moved her eyes back to his. "No more stressing tonight. Darling, I am taking you upstairs to get a shower and to get some sleep." She threw him off when she went up on her toes and kissed him. A tear escaping her eye to slide down her cheek. His mouth marveled in the feel of hers against him.

Taking his hand from her chin he moved it to cup her face and wrapped his other around her back. She moaned into him and linked her arms together around his back. She was forceful, almost like she was trying to forget everything that happened by throwing herself into this. He normally wouldn't mind but this wasn't how he wanted to do this. He almost went too far in the barn earlier, *God had that only been this morning.* It felt like so long ago. Either way, he wanted to do it right the first time and her being overwhelmed was not how he wanted their first time to be remembered.

He took her hands from around him when he pulled back from her lips. Both of them panting, "we need to take this slow." At her look of disappointment, he hurried on, "not that I don't want to darling, because trust me I want to. I just think we should wait a bit." Her cheeks grew an adorable shade of pink and it made his insides quake. "I am going to get you upstairs and cleaned off first. Then I am going to get you in bed." Just the thought of Annette in bed, in his bed, had his cock getting hard. He held back the groan that the image brought up. This woman would be the death of him. Still holding her hands, he pulled her along behind him up the stairs and to his bedroom.

She followed him, not making a sound. Within the silence of the house, the only thing he heard was the blood rushing to his ears and his heart pounding in his chest. Focusing on getting her to the shower was the only thing keeping him from turning around and pressing her up against the wall like every bone in his body wants to do. Holly was in the room across the hall from his, so if she woke up needing something they would know. One less thing to worry about.

Rushing them inside his room he took her to the bathroom. She stood next to him still silent as he turned on the faucet, feeling the water to make sure it was warm. When he looked at her, her lips were still a light pink from their kisses and her eyes had dried but were red from her tears. She wouldn't even look at him. Her eyes solely fixed on the floor and her hair falling around her face.

He stepped up to her, cupped her chin with his palm and had her look up at him. She let out a breath and waited. Waiting for what, he didn't know but he wished she would tell him. Tell him anything that is going on in that pretty little head of hers. They stood there looking at each other for the longest time before he cupped her face in his hands, lightly kissed her and turned to walk out of the bathroom.

****

Annette was so overwhelmed. The spray from the shower did nothing to impede the thoughts running through her head. She felt so bad for putting everyone in this situation. They could have gotten hurt, she could have gotten hurt, holy Hell Holly could have gotten hurt! She turned the heat on higher but even the sting wasn't sinking in. All the guilt and doubt and regret pouring through her veins were all too consuming. She slid down the side of the bathroom stall wall and pulled her knees up to her chest. Her face resting in her palms as she cried. Tears streaming down her face mixing in with all the water. Her sobs were unrecognizable to her own ears. When she had had enough self-pity she wiped her face, slowly stood and stretched out all the tension from her body as best she could. She washed, loving the spicy smell of Austin's soap and shampoo.

She climbed out of the tub to wrap herself in a long white cotton towel. Steam covered the mirror and swam around her as she used another towel to dry off her hair. *Breath in, Breath out* – she reminded herself when she felt like she was going to cry all over again. She chided herself for being like this when she knew life could be worse. At least they were in a house and had people around who cared this time around, instead of the running and worrying she always had to do alone. Quickly she realized she had no clothes in the bathroom to change into. When she felt like she wasn't going to break down she opened the bathroom door to go out into the room to look for her shirt to put back on.

Austin must have been sitting on the bed because when she opened the door he was in the middle of standing. His tall stance and broad frame filling the light spilling out from the bathroom doorway. His eyes roamed her body, so much heat in them that it made her heart beat faster. Their eyes locked a moment later when he made the journey up her body and she saw the hunger in his. She licked her lips and felt a blush creep into her cheeks. He took a few steps forward then stopped to stare at her some more. She knew he could probably see the puffiness of her eyes from all the crying she had done, but if he was concerned, he didn't say anything. Annette felt too exposed and embarrassed at her need for him all of a sudden, she shifted her eyes to the floor. She couldn't look at him anymore, too afraid of what he might see in her eyes. He moved so silently that she didn't even realize he had closed the distance between them till she saw his bare feet stand right in front of hers.

She could smell him, that musty mix of man, cologne and earth. She reveled in the heat she could feel from his body and the chills she got from him being so close to her. He placed his rough hand under her chin and slowly lifted gaze to meet his. His hand caressed her cheek. He spoke so softly that she almost missed it, "So beautiful." Her head tilted into his palm at those words. He leaned in and their mouths met in a tangle of pent up emotions. So much hunger radiated from him that she met it with her own. His other hand snaked around her back to cup her bottom. She moaned at the contact and he used that to claim her mouth with his tongue. Dipping in and tangling with her own. Her arms coming around his shoulders as she lifted onto her tiptoes.

He pulled back before her, both of them panting, to lean his forehead against hers. Annette lightly shook her head side to side, "I am so sorry."

Not breaking contact, he asks, "For what Annette? You don't have anything to be sorry for." He did pull back then, waiting for her to look up at him. When she did she saw so many emotions flicker over his face. She didn't want to admit her fears to him, her anguish over everything. She wanted to go back to kissing him, to lose herself in the feel of him and block everything else out but it was too late for that. She knew it sounded pathetic, her faults over the situation they were all now in, but she couldn't help herself.

"For everything. I hate that I put you in this situation." A soft sob escaping her, "You were right when you said I couldn't escape it, that running wouldn't solve it. I normally would be long gone by now but...but..." He rested his hand under her chin and ran his thumb over her bottom lip. His other hand caressing the outside of her arm. "But what sweetheart?"

"I can't leave you." She sniffed and made a whimper, "I don't want to leave you." Annette couldn't take looking at him anymore. She had to look away and since he wouldn't release his hold on her she tried backing up. Bumping her back into the door jamb made her gasp and push out her chest. The soft fabric of the towel did nothing to stop her nipples from getting hard at the friction or from the feel of him when her chest pushed into him forcibly.

What was she doing? At that moment her cheeks flushed, her body began to ache and she felt like she was going to both flee and melt. She really needed to get her emotions in check or she was going to lose her mind. Austin's right arm left her face and wrapped around her when she collided into him. His left hand flattened on the wall beside her head. His breathing was coming faster and faster, and she wasn't sure if the moan was hers or his.

****

The moan that escaped her lips made him so hard it hurt. He growled then. Low and possessive in his chest. He couldn't deny he wanted her and having her in his arms, up against the wall with only a thin towel separating her skin from him was all but driving him mad with need. Her breathing had her rubbing her nipples against him. He could feel how hard they were, those tight little nubs showing. Her admission of wanting to stay, of not wanting to leave him made his heart want to beat out his chest.

She more than needed him, she wanted him and he loved knowing it. "I never want you to go anywhere either. You have nothing to be sorry for." His voice so steady even he was surprised. He couldn't have sworn his need would come out all shaky as his insides felt at holding back from touching her. When she opened her mouth to reply he spoke again, "None of this is your fault. None of it. Stop blaming yourself for something he did." At that, her mouth clamped shut.

He could tell she was thinking, mulling over his words in her head. Literately saw the storm clouds in her eyes, and he knew she was fighting with the truth and her own feelings. "So, what does that mean for us? Me and Holly?" She clarified. He smiled, "You and Holly are a part of this family now. You have been since Gran first brought you back here." Her smile might have been brief but it was there. Her brain kicking into overdrive with more questions from the look she gave him. She sucked in her bottom lip to chew. *Damn those lips*. So soft and kissable they would drive any man to his knees and he was no exception to that. He moved his hand he had behind her to caress her back, waiting for her to speak.

"So where does that leave you and me?" Her timid words proved to him that she was afraid of the answer. What he said next could either crush her and scare her off or they could reaffirm and comfort her. He knew what he wanted, could already see it in his head but the problem would be getting her to see it.

"Well sweetheart, do you want me?" He needed to hear her say it. To admit it to herself would be a big step. He already knew she didn't want to leave but he knew even if she didn't want him he would still be there to protect her.

"What happened in Texas?" He pulled back. That question took him by surprise. He wasn't expecting to have this conversation now. Letting out a breath of air he motioned for her to sit down on the bed. She shook her head, "I'll stand." Was all she said. He ran his fingers through his hair, "Are you sure you want to talk about this now?"

She stood straighter then, "You want me to answer you but I know nothing of what happened to you. You know all about my relationship problems. I think it is a legitimate question before I give an answer." He couldn't blame her. She wanted to know what happened and he wouldn't lie to her.

He let out a breath, "OK. Here it goes. I worked for a man out in Texas for a while. I went out there to finish up my training for husbandry clinics since I have my degree in agriculture business and production. I knew a guy from college that told me I could stay with him for a summer to get my credits I needed to complete my Bachelor's. I stayed longer because I had met a girl while I was down there, Chasity. "

Chapter 15

His voice got so sad at the mention of the other woman's name that it hurt to listen to. His arms slumped to his sides, his gaze lowered a bit and his voice filled with emotion. "I dated her for the whole summer. We got pretty serious, or at least I thought we did since she agreed to marry me." Annette sucked in her breath. He was going to marry this woman. A woman she didn't even know and for some reason, she couldn't help to feel jealous. This other woman had, had his heart at some point. She didn't like that one little bit.

She had been so lost in her little world for a moment she missed it when he had moved back and sat on the bed. His hands rubbing the stubble on his chin. He rested his face in his hands. His arms on his legs and the downward angle of his face made it hard to hear him, so she moved away from the door and closer to him.

"I found out a week after I had proposed that Chasity was pregnant. I was so happy that we were going to start a life together, have a family, that I never noticed anything was wrong, to begin with. I have never been the kind of guy to be with a lot of girls. I am not made that way."

Her heart started to break when she realized he started to cry. He was wiping at his cheeks and she could tell he was forcing himself to get through this. "You don't have to finish if you don't want to." In fact, she was afraid of where this was going. It made her mad at herself for even asking the question. Somethings should just be left alone. He rapidly shook his head back and forth, "No. You should know this. You are right, I know about you it is only fair you know about me."

She went over to him then. Cradled his head against her stomach. The towel-drying, his tears and his arm pulling her closer as he spread his legs to let her in. The embrace more for comfort that sexual need but she still got tingles being this close to him. Running a finger through his chestnut hair had helped steady his breathing she noticed. Allowing him time to breathe before going on.

"I found out about the pregnancy because one of the cooks was talking about it. I assumed she was going to surprise me with it, that is until I found out she made an appointment at an abortion clinic." Annette tensed against him. This other woman was going to get rid of his baby? Who could do something like that? He wasn't just going to dump her, surely, she knew that since he wanted to marry her right? "I confronted her when she was getting ready to leave. We had it out in the front of the house, in view of everyone. I asked her how she could get rid of our baby and that is when she told me it wasn't mine."

She couldn't help the words, "Oh My God," that blurted out of her mouth. Couldn't hold them back even if she wanted to. The shock of his words, this story he was telling her, had her heartbreaking for him. He nodded, "Yea that is about it. She informed me then that she had been seeing another one of the ranch hands while she had been seeing me. She didn't realize how serious I was about her till I asked her to marry me and by then it was too late. Oh, she tried to tell me that when I asked her she had ended it with the other guy but by then I was so ashamed and dumbfounded that I couldn't speak. Turns out she never ended it with the other ranch hand. That girl didn't even tell him he was going to be a father. She went to that clinic without even telling him. He found out four days later, the day I was leaving because the clinic called the house and the cook answered. The cook, Missy, talks a lot. Not much is kept secret around here." He tried to chuckle at that. She wasn't going to tell him he failed miserably at it, so she let it slide. "I didn't stay around for that fight. Last, I heard from my friend Chasity moved out of state with another guy, and the ranch hand went to live with his cousin in Ohio. Funny how things work out." She felt him tug on the towel and she looked down at his eyes. They were rimmed in liquid and so full of, is that love? No, it couldn't be, could it? He had only known her for a short while, but if she knew herself she would say what she saw and felt for herself was love.

"Now you know. So I will ask you again, do you want me?" His words so soft and his gaze fell to her mouth. The darkening of his irises made her let out a sigh. "Yes." Was all she could get out. The one word so full of meaning. "Yes what?" he retorted, raising an eyebrow. A sly smile creeping into his voice and on his face. She matched his with her own. "Yes, I want you," was all she needed to whisper.

His mouth took hers. Her toes curled and goosebumps crept over her skin. She embraced it, all of it. The feel of his lips, the hunger in his kiss, the wispier fabric between them rubbing against her skin, his hands feeling from her face down to her ass and then sliding to the V between her legs. Everywhere he touched her it lit her skin ablaze with need. Tingles shot through her body and goosebumps covered her flesh.

"So sexy," he murmured against her lips. She pulled back, the top of his head reaching just above her nose when she leaned down to look at him. No one ever made her feel so, but right now him saying it and the look in his eyes, his hands caressing her like he couldn't get enough was all proof of how he felt. "You are mine Annette, sweetheart, and I am yours. Your place is with me. There is no more leaving, no more running. Do you understand? I will put a ring on that finger if you don't get how much you mean to me."

Annette took a step back, "Is that a proposal?" The words he spoke excited her but that last part had her mind reeling. Did he really just propose to her like that? He rubbed her arm, "No. When I propose, I will do it properly. A ring and everything. I am just making a point. If that is what it will take for you to understand I am serious about you and Holly, then I will. I want you, both of you to stay with me. Annette, you complete me."

She had tears in her eyes when he finished. His hand snaked up to rub one away. "Shhh," was all he got out before he pulled her in to kiss her again. This time more slowly and passionately. He tugged at the towel till it fell, pooling at her feet. She heard him suck in a breath the moment the towel hit the floor. Her cheeks flushed and her skin heated. Embarrassment flooding her and she wrapped her hands around herself.

****

Only light from the bathroom spilled into the room giving him just enough vision to see. She was beautiful but her hands covered herself almost instantly. He wanted to see her, he was a man after all with a beautiful woman, his beautiful woman, standing in front of him. He wasn't going to deny he wanted to see her, all of her and so much more. "What's wrong?" Trying to make the question as gentle as he could with all the need he was feeling. A bit proud of himself he got it out without his voice cracking. She looked at him still covering herself, her eyes a mixture of lust and worry. Why was she worried? He already told her he wanted her, heck she could see he needed her if she only looked down at his crotch. The material of his jeans straining against his hard erection.

She didn't say anything, just shook her head and slowly moved her hands to her sides. Now that he could see her, all of her, he knew why she worried. Scars and skin discoloration colored dotted throughout her upper and lower abdomen. He had no doubt it would go around to her backside. Rage filled him then, hot burning rage. He knew she had suffered but he didn't know it was anything like this. No wonder she was always afraid to be touched, but she had come alive in his arms, heck they both had. He placed a hand over one of her scars and rubbed gently.

Their gazes locked and no one said a word for a while. He had almost given up on her speaking when she trembled a moment later, "I told you there were many fights. This is the result of them. They don't hurt anymore, just some leftover reminders." The pain in her voice had his gut twisting. He pulled her to him and had her sitting sideways on his lap. His hand running through her hair and rubbing her back. "You are beautiful. All of you." He rubbed his hand over her discolored skin, "every inch of you turns me on and the sooner you realize that the sooner I can appreciate every inch of you."

Her moan had his hips rubbing into her ass. Her mouth found his ear and suckled. He grabbed her legs, turned her to straddle him, while he grabbed her ass and suckled on her neck. A growl from deep in his chest rose to his throat. Her voice a purr against his ear, "you have too many clothes on."

He had her laughing really hard when he quickly moved her off him to stand and start pulling off his clothes. Falling to the floor when he tried to take his boots off and was failing. He had to slow down to get them off and pull off his pants. Standing in only his boxers he finally caught his breath and smiled. "Is this good enough?"

She sat up, wiping the tears from her eyes due to laughing so hard, and put a finger to her chin in mock thinking. Her finger fell from her chin and her head swayed from side to side, "still too many clothes," she said.

She had to know how sexy she looked just laying back across his bed. Hair resting about her, her breast on display, even her scars could not hide her wonderful curves and smooth skin that went even between her legs. She looked so perfect in his bed, where she belonged. The sight of her there felt so right he knew he had to do everything he could to keep her there with him. No matter what obstacles they faced later, he would do everything he could to make sure she never faced a problem alone again.

****

She felt exposed but for the first time, in a very long time, she believed the words he had said.

The man standing in front of her wanted her, even with all her marred skin, he still wanted her and she felt sexy for it. The room was a little chilled but she didn't mind since her skin felt like it was on fire under his gaze. He slowly pulled down his boxers, a contrast to his early fumbles of haste in getting his clothes off. His cock bounced when it was freed. All of him now standing at attention and she drank in the sight of him. Tan, hard muscle with corded arms and legs. All of him screamed man not boy and she loved looking at every inch.

Licking her lips in anticipation she crooked her finger at him to come to her. He walked over to her and completely covered her body with his, taking her mouth with such fierceness that it stole her breath. To be fair she wanted him just as much as he said he wanted her, she just needed to hear it. When she did it made her whole body relax enough to enjoy what was happening between them. Always being afraid and having to be on alert to protect her daughter had her nerves frayed. Now, with this man in her arms on top of her, she was giving in to her wanton needs.

A tangle of hands touching, mouths licking and sucking, and moans of pleasure eloped them for a few moments. "I need to taste you," he said as she slid her hands between then to grip him. She whimpered as he slid down her, trailing kisses from her mouth, down her neck, over her stomach and resting between her thighs. He parted her legs further, pushing them higher in the air. "Spread wider for me beautiful. Yes, just like that." Anette felt a light flicker of a finger on her clit and jumped at the contact. "You are so beautiful. Such a pretty pink and already so wet for me." She had never had someone talk to loving and dirty to her before during intimacy. It both had her nervous and so turned on. Her need showing in how wet she was getting.

He slipped one finger deep inside her while his other hand still held onto her leg. She moaned as his thrusting increased in pace. "So, sexy. Yes, darling, that's it, moan for me." She didn't even realize she was doing it till he said something. Not having sex in so long and now being touch and exposed like this had her on edge. She wanted him inside her before she came. "Please," she begged. His strokes never faltered, "What baby? What do you need?" She shuddered at his words and the feel of his fingers filling her. "I want you inside me. Please." She said again.

"Soon sweetheart, soon." Was all he said before he took his fingers out, making her feel so empty where he had just been. He placed both hands around her thighs and pulled her closer to his waiting mouth. Her whole body tensed when he first stroked his tongue over her swollen clit. Then relaxed as he repeated it over and over in circles. She moaned loudly and grabbed the bedsheets. He never let up on the pressure of his strokes. His hands snaked up and started playing with her nipples. Rubbing and lightly pinching to send tingles all the way down to between her legs. So much sensation all at once had her eyes rolling back and her head falling onto the mattress. Her breathing became harsher and her climax built all too soon. When he growled into her, the vibration sent her over the edge. Her back arched, her hips bucked and she screamed out her pleasure. Pushing her pussy into his face so hard she might have been worried about him not being able to breathe if she could process anything at that moment.

When her last waves of orgasm rushed over her, her body relaxed back down on the mattress. Austin sat up on his elbows and wiped her wetness from his face. "You taste so fucking good, I needed that." A soft cry escaped her lips, her body tired and sated from her release. She felt him shift off the bed. Heard him walk to the nightstand and open a drawer. The crinkle of a condom filled her ears and she opened her eyes to look over at him as he shut the drawer. He turned to the bed and she flipped herself onto her stomach, her legs bent at the knees in the air. She knew her hair must have been a mess and she didn't care. "Uh-huh," she said grabbing his thigh and pulling him toward her before he could open the condom.

"You don't get to taste and I can't. It's my turn."

****

God what this woman does to him! Those soft pouty lips, the taste of her still in his mouth, and now she was asking to take him in her mouth like a vixen. She was amazing. He saw her hungrily lick her lips and was surprised at her eagerness even after he had made her cum all over his face. How she had come apart under his tongue! It was the most beautiful thing he had ever seen and he wanted more of it, of her.

He moved closer to the bed, his erection pointing directly at her. She looked up at him as he pulled her hair away from her face and held it at the nape of her neck. He needed this, her as much as he needed to breathe. Nothing about her was timid as she slid her tongue over his hard shaft while still staring up at him. "You're so big and hard," she murmured against him. The vibration making his cock more engorged. She stroked his balls in her hand and crawled further to him, reminding him of a cat. She purred like one too he remembered.

"I want you to thrust down my throat."

Those words drove him insane. The sultriness of her voice mixed with the look of desire in her eyes almost sent him over the edge. Gritting his teeth hard to fight the urge to cum when she swallowed him wholly in her mouth. The softness of her mouth and lips against him had him cursing, "Fuck baby." He sucked in a breath as she suctioned onto him, still fisting her hair as he guided her. With his other hand, he leaned over and grabbed her ass giving it a light smack that echoed in the stillness of the room. Her purr of pleasure vibrated against him and he knew she liked it.

"Like that, do you?" She didn't have to answer; his question was answered when he dipped his hand between her ass cheeks and found her dripping wet. His fingers stroking in and out of her while she sucked on him harder and faster. She whimpered against him when he withdrew his fingers and pulled his hand away. His other hand making her head stay still as he plunged his cock in and out of her mouth.

A few fast strokes and he pulled out of her mouth. "Sweetheart, you are… you're so amazing. I need to be inside of you, I want to be in you when I cum." He was surprised out solid his voice was when all he felt like doing was roar out and flip her over and claim her, hard. But her would take this slow. As slow as he could make it, anyway. Watching as Annette sat back on her knees on the bed, he tore the condom open and sheathed himself. She was patiently waiting for him to come to her and he loved knowing she wanted him just as much as he wanted her. Her need has matched his beat for beat and he wasn't going to let up.

Her lips so full of kissing and their sucking they made his cock twitch. Her breast so full and taunt had his heart skipping beats. Her pussy was dripping wet, he could see the glistening proof running down the inside of her thighs and he growled. Her eyes went wide at the sound and she stiffened. "Is something wrong," she asked.

He had to smile because he couldn't believe she thought something was wrong. He knew he had to be up soon to take care of the ranch and he already missed her. The only thing wrong was him not wanting to leave her to work, but if he had to he would make sure she was completely satisfied first. That is one thing he could do and he planned on doing it, even if it meant he was going to be dragging tomorrow.

He laid down on the bed, stretching out with his head on the pillow. Annette was still crouched back on her legs at his side. "Nothing is wrong darling unless you don't come here." At that, she relaxed and moved over to him. He caressed her cheek and pulled her lips down to him. He would never get tired of kissing her. All soft and sweet and his. He moved her to straddle his lap, her opening hovering just above the head of his cock.

"If you want me to stop you better tell me now," he bent his knees, pressing his ass flat against the mattress and separating his cock from her opening just enough, "I won't be able to stop if I go anything else." Her hands rested on his chest, rubbed and played with the soft speckle of hair there. "I never asked you to stop."

That was all he needed to hear before grabbing her hips and plunging himself into her. He took her hard and fast, thrusting as she screamed out her pleasure. She erupted over him, her nails digging into his chest. "You are mine sweetheart," he left no room for doubt as he gave one last thrust deep inside her, the walls of her pussy squeezing him with her orgasm, and exploded. He saw dots of white snake across his vision as his cum filled the condom. Her breast brushed against his chest as she leaned over to collapse on top of him.

"So that is what I have been missing." He gave a low chuckle at her words. "Wow," she stated before yawning. He felt her nuzzle into him, "that good," he asked. "Mmmmhmmm," was her reply.

He rubbed her back and moved her hair out of her face and off her neck. "I am gonna get cleaned off, you get comfortable under the covers." He slipped out of her and she whined. "I'll be right back," he kissed her head of mussed hair. She was so gorgeous and sexy with that *just been fucked* look. She seemed to accept that answer because she climbed up the bed, pulled the covers over her bare skin and snuggled into the pillows.

He came back out of the bathroom a few minutes later after a quick shower and saw her already asleep on the bed. How had he lived without this woman, his woman, before now, he wondered? His life before now seemed so dull in comparison to having her in it.

After a quick check of the house and Holly, who was still asleep in her bed, he finally allowed himself to crawl into bed beside Annette. She snuggled right up onto his chest and he felt pride in his ability to wear her out. His arm snuggly around her he rubbed her side. His hand gliding across a few different scars on her side. He swore to her and Holly nothing bad would ever happen like what they had endured again, not while he was alive to protect her. He turned and set his alarm for three hours from now and turned to kiss her head one more time before falling into a deep sleep next to her. His dreams filled with every hope for their future.

Chapter 16

The breeze sweeping through her hair and the light coming in from the open window warming her cheek greeted her as she woke. Annette swiped her hair away from her eyes and wiped her mouth, embarrassment flushing her cheeks as she realized she had been drooling on the pillow she laid on. Looking over she realized she was alone in the big bed. Now that it was daylight she could take in her surroundings. Austin's bedroom was about the same size as the one she had stayed in, in the house but the shape was a little different with a window bench seat and wider. Masculine colors of blues and reds filled the room, a big flat-screen TV on the far wall and next to it was three dressers. The bed took up a portion of the room with its stocky wooden frame and matching nightstands.

The bed all but swallowed her with its massive size but she didn't mind one bit until she had to get out of it. Her feet dangled over the side and she had to scooch herself over to hop down. This being one of those times where her size really made her think about wearing heels, but then she remembered her motto. "I like being small, it means all the tall people get to do things for me," she chimed to herself. Padding across the floor she went to the bathroom. After relieving herself and brushing her teeth with toothpaste she put on her finger, she looked at herself in the mirror. Her hair was a rustled mess that she tried to tame with her fingers, and Austin's shirt did nothing to hide her frame beneath it.

He had touched every inch of her, even her scars and had not said anything negative about them.

Even though Terry had given her those scars, he had chided her on them over and over again in the past. He always got mad when another wound never went away because it made her more unappealing to him. The same feeling of shame washed over her, only to be pushed back by rage. It wasn't her fault she told herself. She realized that a while ago and learned to love herself, but because of the things he had drilled into her she always doubted anyone else would ever look past all the painful reminders. She always felt like she would never let another person see her naked because what if he'd been right, that she was ugly and unattractive, but with Austin, it wasn't like that at all.

He never said anything negative about her marred nude flesh. He couldn't stop touching her and those things he said, the things he did with his hands and his mouth. Her body tingled at the memory. She padded away from the counter and pulled on her pants from yesterday. She would have to talk to him later about what their next steps would be for their future. She knew there would be, he had said she wasn't going anywhere, that he had wanted her and that she was his. She didn't need to hear more to know he was keeping her, keeping them. She and Holly were a package deal and she would talk with Holly about it before she made it official, but she already knew her daughter had fallen for the man too.

She came out of the bathroom and was just about to go downstairs when she noticed a flower and note laying on the pillow that Austin must have slept on. She walked over to it and lifted the single dandelion up smiling to herself. *This was an odd flower for the morning after, heck for any day*, she noted to herself. She picked up the small note and read:

> I wanted you to rest. So beautiful and peaceful.
> I will miss you but I will see you for lunch.
> I already made my wish and got it,
> thought you'd like a chance to blow and make one for yourself.
> Your Cowboy Always,
> A.

There was no way she could have felt happier than at that moment. She was so satisfied and felt fulfilled that she actually didn't know what to do with all this energy. Her smile hurt her face and she giggled to herself like a schoolgirl. Taking in a breath she drew the dandelion to her lips. Silently she made a wish, counted to three and blew. All the seeds flew about the room leaving the stalk empty and her heart full of hope.

She all but skipped down to breakfast. Her whole demeanor felt light and lifted. There might be danger lurking about from her ex but she wasn't going to dwell on that. Not after the life-altering night, she had just had. Holly was sitting in a chair at the island drinking a sippy cup and a stack of pancakes sitting in front of her. "Now you make sure to eat as much as you can. Do you want some…" Carolynn stopped what she was saying when Annette walked in. The other woman looked her up and down approvingly like she knew what had happened last night and she approved. She may or may not know, either way, it wouldn't change her mood any. "Look what the coyote dragged in."

Annette just kept smiling as she took a seat next to her daughter. "Good Morning to you too,' Annette replied as she started cutting up Holly's pancakes. Her daughter giggling and hugging her.

"Morning," Carolynn all but huffed, "it is almost lunchtime. You must have really needed that rest." Carolynn did her clucking as she turned to grab another plate of pancakes and sat them in front of her. "I already ate. I am gonna clean up some of these dishes before making lunch for the men and then I am going to do some laundry. Lord knows it never ends with all the dirtballs we have around here." Annette and Holly chuckled as the older woman threw her hands in the air mocking exasperation at having to cater to other people. Annette knew it was just an act because the other woman loved doing things for other people. It was one of the first things she noticed about the other woman's character and was so endearing.

"It can't be that late." Sure enough, as she looked at the clock on the wall it said 10:45 PM. She really had slept. Before the other woman could reply she added, "do you need any help with anything?"

Carolynn just said over her shoulder, "No. Just eat and make sure that little one eats too." Annette heard the dishes start clanking around in the sink before turning to Holly. Her daughter already shoveling what she could into her mouth and missing pieces that were falling to the floor. She didn't have syrup on hers, just butter and it was melting everywhere. Normally she would be softly chiding her for making such a mess but she didn't feel as stressed as she normally did. She would say it was just because of a night of great sex but that wouldn't be totally true. Yes, the sex had been great but it also had to do with the man that was now and would hopefully forever be, a part of their lives from now on.

"Slow down baby," she wiped at Holly's mouth with a napkin, "Do you want any syrup after we clean this mess up?" Holly shook her head no and picked at a piece of fallen pancake off her shirt. "Mommy, are we going to be leaving again?" Annette's head snapped up and hit the bottom of the counter from her crouching position on the floor while cleaning up some pancake mess. At the same time, Carolynn had whipped around, her soapy hands dripping on the front of her apron. Annette rubbed the top of her head at the dulling pain from her collision with the counter as she stood. Both sets of eyes boring into her and waiting on an answer.

She felt a pang of sadness and guilt because her daughter was expecting it. Whenever Terry had come around or shown up, they left. Hell, they left if there was even a chance of him showing up. She knew her daughter was just asking a simple question, but she also knew the answer she was waiting to hear and it was drastically different this time around. She wanted to make it clear but also make sure her daughter was ok with it.

Those big hazel eyes staring straight into her with so much hope her heart began to ache. "Is that what you want to do munchkin?" Holly was already shaking her messy hair before Annette could even get the whole sentence out. "No Mommy. I like it here." She pulled her in for a hug and her daughter leaned into her. This hug was as much a comfort to Holly as it was to her. Carolynn visibly relaxing, a smile stretching across her face before she turned back around and began her washing once again.

"I like it here too munchkin," she said pulling back to cup her daughter's chin in both hands. "We will be here for a long time." *I hope.* That last part she kept to herself but she couldn't help thinking it. Something usually came up and they had to leave. She really hoped this time didn't just feel different but was different. Her hands dropped as Holly turned to go back to eating her pancakes. Her daughter seemed happier just from the confirmation that this time would be different.

But I'm still worried, she thought. Worried that something more drastic might happen, that someone will get hurt badly this time, or that Austin or Carolynn might not want them hereafter it is all said and done. She was worried she might become more of a complication then a relief. The sound of dishes crashing had her pushing these unnerving thoughts from her head and focusing on what was going on around her.

****

Austin's heart leaped into his throat at the sound of a loud crash. All the men were starting to come in to get lunch before they headed out to search. They had slowly started arriving a half-hour ago, Tony brought three of his deputies, Hugh brought four of his ranch hands, and Austin had asked five of his own hands to help in the search. They had all huddled at the bottom of the porch steps when they heard the sound inside the house and every man went rushing up the steps towards the noise.

Austin and Tony were the first ones in the kitchen followed by the other thirteen men. "What is going on in here," Tony yelled, his hand clamping down on his Smith and Wesson 40 caliber instinctively. Holly was on the stool right in front of him, the remnants of her breakfast covering her shirt. Annette and Carolynn were by the sink and some broken dishes covered the floor at their feet. They both looked like a deer in the headlights as they turned towards him and the other men.

He would have thought it was funny if his heart wasn't still pounding in his chest. Carolynn spoke first, "What are all of you doing in my kitchen traipsing mud everywhere?" Her hands flew to her hips. Becoming exasperated at the lack of an answer of what was going on he put his palms up, "we heard a crash and came in. What is going on? Is everything ok?" He hadn't even noticed the smile on Annette's face till she snorted into her arm. Tony let out a small chuckle next to him. "I dropped the dishes. There was a damn mouse in my sink. Looks like we need a house cat or an exterminator. I'll let you decide." His Gran started clucking her tongue which she usually did when she was flustered or thinking, or both. The sound gave a sense of normalcy and made him relax some. They were under no real threat.

"Now get everyone out of my house this instant or else no one eats. You think my floors clean themselves!?"

"They would if you would let me get you one of those floor cleaning robots." He retorted as everyone started heading back out the door. Annette still smiling. A smile she only seemed to be focusing on him and he was not arguing about it. Damn, she looked so sexy in his shirt and half tasseled. The glow in her cheeks had him remembering last night and he felt himself grow hard. The friction in his pants not fully welcomed since it would become uncomfortable walking around outside. He would have to get used to this if this is what looking at her was going to do to his libido.

He had not heard anything his Gran had replied to his comment, drowning everyone else out until Tony was tugging on his sleeve towards the door. He shook his head to bring him out of his thoughts, "Alright I 'm coming," he said following Tony out of the door. He could hear the snickering behind him in the kitchen but couldn't make any of it out. Holly had run after them before him and Tony made it out the door, "-Stin I have to tell you! Mommy said we stay!" She was a mess and her hair was everywhere. Bits of whatever she had been eating everywhere but the genuine excitement on her face and the meaning of her words had his mind reeling. "You are staying?" He asked.

Her head bobbing up and down and her hands clapping. His smile reached his eyes. "That's great munchkin. I am so glad." He saw Annette making her way down the hallway with a tray of sandwiches. When she reached the end, Austin stood.

Clearing his throat behind him Tony offered to take the tray out to the porch. He had forgotten the other man was there until he spoke up but he knew he did it to give them a minute. Annette knelt down to Holly, "Baby go in the kitchen and get cleaned up some, please."

Without another word Holly ran back down the hallway to the kitchen, leaving Austin alone with her. The goofy smile must have still been on his face when she finally looked at him because she tilted her head in question, "what are you looking at me like that for?" He couldn't hold back, he closed the distance between them and pulled her in for a hug. Her arms wrapped around his middle and she giggled. "What is this for," she sighed into him.

"A little birdie said you were staying. I am just showing you how much I agree with this idea." He pulled back, "Is that so," she said more than asked. He nodded and pulled her in for a deep lingering kiss. This kiss conveyed more than just lust and need. This kiss, he knew, was a kiss to welcome her home.

She was home and she was staying. His veins sang inside him at the prospect of her always being here, in his arms, and in this home. "We will celebrate properly when we can have everyone over." He said in her ear His skin felt on fire when she nibbled his ear trailing down to his collarbone. "We can celebrate privately later too." His voice came out more gravely then he meant to. His length still hard inside his jeans as he pressed it up against her belly. He heard the tiny gasp of air she let out at the contact and he grinned in her hair.

He could have stayed there teasing forever but reality set in when his Gran came walking down the hallway with another tray of sandwiches. "Are you two gonna help or are you just gonna stand in my way," she said as she tapped her foot behind them. Austin saw his smile mirrored back at him from Annette as she spoke, "Here I'll take those." Grabbing the tray from Carolynn she turned right back around to get more things from the kitchen. "And I'll finish this later," He said so only she could hear before he turned and took the tray outside.

The men didn't say anything to him as he walked back out on the porch. All of them in their own conversations about their day to day lives. The women brought out trays of drinks before heading back in the house to clean up the mess the men had left in their haste to find out what was going on earlier. As the men ate their lunch they discussed where they were going to look. Tony handed out copies of mug shots of Terry so everyone knew who they were looking for. The men became more serious as they were wrapping up their meals. Protecting his family at the forefront of his mind when all the men's heads shot up towards the barn.

Loud whinnies and noises were coming from inside. Austin heard banging and sounds of distress. As the men ran over and opened the barn door four barn cats came rushing out past them. All the men had their guns in hand as they peered inside to see what had the animals spooked. Snakes. Snakes everywhere. "What the hell," Hugh yelled from somewhere behind him and he had to agree he was thinking the same thing.

"Those are copperheads. Someone dumped all of them." Tony turned to face the men, "Any of you see anyone around the barn?" They all shook their heads. *Of course, they hadn't seen anyone*, he thought, they were all just talking and eating. No one was paying any attention to the barn.

The stall doors were solid wood and went all the way to the floor. This kept the snakes out of the horse stalls but didn't stop them from scaring the poor creatures. One of the men from Hugh's crew spoke up, "we all know who did this. A few of us better start walking around. He couldn't have gotten far." Tony and Austin nodded. "Alright, Hugh and your men survey around the barn. I am going to take my deputies and Austin to start walking the fields. Austin," he looked at him then, "you mind if your men stay here and get these wrangled up?"

"Works for me, Sherriff." All the men broke up after that, going where they were told. Austin walked over to the field where he already had some of the horses saddled up for his men to ride and motioned for the other men to mount up. Riding across the fields would help them cover more ground than just walking it. They all knew the man they were looking for could be anywhere by now.

They were down in the south pasture staring at open land when he got a radio call stating the snakes were all rounded up and disposed of. None of the horses had been hurt but one of the cats had been found deceased outside the barn, having been bitten. One of his men found a knapsack on the floor and Tony told them not to touch it. He would collect it when he got back. It could have fingerprints on it and they all knew whose fingerprints they would probably find. Before ending the call, Austin told his men to saddle up and start grazing the north pasture to cover that area.

Just when they were about to turn back towards the house one of Tony's deputies called over his shoulder. Deputy Yates, who barley ever spoke when Austin was around the other man, said: "Any of you see something red over there?" He pointed to a tree that was at the edge of an embankment to a stream. The other men shook their heads at first but Austin just stared harder. Even though the sun had started to set, they had been out there for over an hour and a half, it was still hard to see with the light shining in his eyes. He pulled his hat down lower to shield his vision some and then he saw it. A light splattering of red covered the ground around the tree. From this distance, it either was a massacre or there was something else all over the ground.

"We'd better go check it out," Austin whistled to his horse and gave a slight kick to get him to move. The other men followed close behind without saying another word the whole way. The feeling of dread filling him the closer they got but when they came closer Austin pulled to a stop. The other men went past him before they realized he wasn't moving anymore and they turned around to meet him.

"I am going to dismount here and walk over. If there are any foot or hoof prints I want to be able to see them." The other nodded agreement and dismounted together. Fanning out before moving closer proved to be helpful because Tony yelled out he found hoof prints. He pulled out his phone and took photos while they scanned the area. He also got shots of footprints as they got closer to the scene.

"Damn," Officer Yates said just before Austin said, "Fuck." They stood staring at a mess of bottles, broken glass, and the red they saw earlier was blood. The tree had all kinds of animals hanging upside down, their bodies were either skinned or their throats slit. After Tony took more pictures with his phone, they walked around more to inspect the surroundings. A fire pit was down by the water and a makeshift tent. The inspection of the tent turned up nothing.

Officer Ferrell, who had not said a word the whole time spoke up, "You might want to get over here." Austin and Tony rushed up the embankment to meet the other men where officer Ferrell stood on the opposite side of the tree holding a sack. "What'd you find Ferrell," Tony asked.

"You're not going to like this," he said tipping the bag over and letting all the contents fall onto the ground. "Looks like your guy has been busy for a while." Photos of Annette and Holly littered the ground along with papers and two notebooks. Austin bent down to pick up some of the photos. Some were taken closer up than others but in all of them showed it was obvious objects of the photos were unaware they were being photographed. Holly was so young in some of them and in others it was more recent. Austin's blood ran cold when he noticed how recent somewhere. He picked up one of Annette walking through town with Carolynn. A happy Holly next to the two women. Then there was one of Austin and Annette in an intimate embrace in the barn. On the back of it was scribbled, *WHORE*.

His teeth gritted and anger started to rise in his chest. The sun was rapidly going down now so it made it a bit harder to see the contents still laying around the ground. Officer Ferrell and Yates started to deposit the contents on the ground back into the sac. Before they were done Tony's, radio chirped and everyone stood still. Annie, the dispatcher, and department part-time receptionist's high-pitched voice rang through the device.

"Sherriff Townsend."

"Go for the Sherriff."

"We have a 1010 in progress at the Rayne Falls Ranch."

Every man held their breath, solely focused on the radio Tony held in his hand. Austin's stomach did a lurch and quickly rose to his feet.

"I'm on the homestead with the deputies now." There had never been a more deafening sound as all of them waiting for the radio to click back on.

"Do you need me to call the next town over for backup Sherriff?"

"I'll take care of it, Annie. Thanks." He replaced his radio to his belt buckle. Austin was already on his horse and riding off before the other men reached theirs. He heard their voices in the background behind him but he was more concerned with getting home, back to his family and whatever was going on. He didn't know what a 1010 was but if Annie was calling something bad had to be going on and he wanted to get there as fast as he could.

Chapter 17

All those men outside had been there to help her and Holly. She felt safe and loved and comforted in a way she had never felt before. When everyone had come charging into the kitchen she had known then and there nothing bad would happen to them. She knew Austin wouldn't let it. A rush of heat washed over her at the thought of him and she had to clamp her mouth shut to avoid a moan. It came out more of a groan instead and Carolynn had turned her head towards her. The other woman had been putting the rest of the leftover sandwiches back into the fridge for later.

"What's the matter, dear?" The other woman looked her from head to toe.

"Nothing," she muttered. Just then Holly came running back in from the bathroom. Her hands and top were all wet and her hair had droplets of water in it. "Oh, my goodness. What did you do in there?" Annette picked her up and wipe some of the water from her hair. "Holy oh mighty child did you swim in that bathroom?" Carolynn chimed in.

Holly just giggled excitedly for all the attention she was getting, "I all clean!" she yelled to them both. "I all clean," she said again for emphasis. Holly nuzzled her nose to Annette obviously proud of herself for at least trying.

"Yes, you did," she agreed. At least she did to an extent. "I am going to help you clean up the kitchen and then I am going to take this little one with me to go wash up properly and change into normal clothes."

Tongue clicking soon followed her response and she half expected it to, "I thought Austin didn't want you going out to that house by yourself? I think it would be wise to stay here till they get back." Carolynn now was across the island from her and staring her in the eyes. The other woman looked at all the mother figure she wished she would have had now. Maybe she did in a way through her.

With a smile and a nod of her head, "He did but Holly can't stay a mess all day and we don't know when the men will be back." They heard them run off the porch and assumed the commotion with the horses was them mounting up. That was over an hour ago. "Besides, I need clothes for me and her if we are to stay here for a few days. Oh, and my laptop so I can get some work done." She heard a sigh and the other woman dropped her hands to her side. Annette knew she was just being concerned for her and she loved her for it.

"I guess that makes sense. You better call Austin before you leave though. He needs to know what is going on. I don't need him coming back here to find you left and then give me an ear full. No, I don't." The other woman pointed to the phone on the wall. Annette was surprised people still had the older machines but she also felt a bit of nostalgia at it.

"I promise." After than another half hour went by with them both cleaning up the kitchen and the hallway mess then men made earlier when they ran in. She was tired, mostly from trying to keep Holly off of the furniture since she still had a sticky mess on her. Annette rolled her eyes as Carolynn reminded her to call Austin before she went out.

Grabbing the phone off the wall she already had a speech in her mind she was going to say if he objected to her going, but she never got to say any of it. The call went straight to voicemail and she left a voicemail explaining why she was going to her house and that she wouldn't be long. Hanging up she felt off. Austin never had his phone off, that she could think of. Maybe his phone died or he did it to lessen the distraction while he was out? Either way, she turned to let Carolynn know about the phone call and grabbed Holly before walking out the door.

The walk to the cottage wasn't far but it felt eerie. Almost as if someone was watching her the whole time. She kept turning around scanning the area but saw nothing, not even the men who should be searching. She tried reasoning that it must be one of the men from the search party since there were a lot of them, and kept walking.

"Mommy," Holly asked.

"Yes, baby."

"Why is the front door open?" Holly said pointing to the wide-open door. For a moment, she froze in place. Worry and concern pouring from her with a tinge of fear. Then she remembered that the men were in her place last night and sort of relaxed, as much as she could while still feeling like someone was watching her.

"Austin and his friends must have left it open while they were looking around, yesterday baby. It's ok. We are just going to get some clothes, change you and were going back to the big house. OK?"

"OK, Mommy," Holly said skipping next to her as they started moving again.

She couldn't shake this feeling but pushed it aside when they made their way up the porch and walked in. Holly ran up the stairs and to her room. She tried keeping up with her but wasn't fast enough. Holly was in her room pulling open her own drawers when Annette came up. Pulling out matching clothes Annette took her daughter to the bathroom and cleaned her up before changing her. A matching white unicorn shirt and pink pants brought out the color in her daughter's eyes.

After putting Holly's shoes on and grabbing some more clothes for the other house, Annette went into her room to change. Holly did not leave her side once since coming upstairs. She grabbed some of her own clothes and threw all of them into a duffle bag she found in the back of her closet. Feeling satisfied she found everything she needed they both went down the stairs. Holly stopped at the bottom and Annette bumped into her.

"Oomph," she said at the impact. She was going to say something but Holly's face had her stopping what she was going to say. "Holly what's wrong." She followed the pointed finger Holly put up to the Livingroom. Sitting on the couch was someone she hoped they would never see again, Terry.

****

Annette squelched down a shriek. Words came out sounding more confident than she felt. "What are you doing here?"

He moved his eyes around the room and gestured the same with his hand. "The whole time. You didn't even notice me when you came in precious." That nickname he had given her always made her feel sick to her stomach and this time was no exception. He liked pet names during intercourse too and it just made her skin crawl every time she heard one. "Hi sweetness," he said to Holly, "Come give me a kiss."

Anette moved her hand to Holly's shoulder, nudging her behind her. "Terry, what do you want?" Her heart was racing now, she could feel it practically beat out of her chest but she had to reign it in or she would overreact and that could lead to worse situations. She knew from past experience. Terry didn't say anything at first. He turned, placing one mud and, *was that blood on his jeans?* It was dark and red but she couldn't be sure. One leg on the floor the other on the couch to effectively look her direction he said, "You're my woman and that's my brat," he pointed from her to Holly, "I came to bring you home."

Holly was holding onto Annette's shirt from behind but peaked around her to say, "we stay here." Terry's face scowled at her words and he got a harshness to his features that was never a good sign.

"You are coming with me sweetness. My you are getting so ripe." She wanted to throw up at the words. Instead, she gagged in her mouth and tried to stand taller. "We are home Terry," she said to him. The look on his face getting darker and his eyes narrowed, "we are not going anywhere. As Holly said we are staying. Why don't you just go." Her own voice sounded different. More calm, surer then what her body was feeling at that moment.

Terry stood at that remark and Annette realized it had to be blood on his pants and his shirt. It splattered out from the middle of his clothes and covered over some of the mud. She shivered at the sight of him and not in a good way. Not like she had with Austin in front of her. Austin, oh how she wished he would just walk in through that door, but no, he wouldn't. He doesn't even know they are out here.

She dropped the bag and pulled Holly flush against her back as Terry began moving toward them. His booted feet caked with mud pounding the floorboards. Every time a boot hit the floor matted mud flew off them. His breathing was more harsh with every step he took and her own was coming in short waves trying to make sense of the situation she was now in.

She couldn't let him get to Holly no matter what happened to her. She edged herself toward the door, effectively moving Holly along with her. She was almost there when she heard, "tsk, tsk, tsk." Come from him. A finger-wagging in front of his own face. "Don't do anything stupid now." He looked at where her hands were behind her. "You stop moving or I am going to have to get physical." She stopped at that remark. Her feet planted in place.

She could feel Holly behind her, clinging to her. Her hands started to shake and she knew her daughter was scared too. She could feel it. She heard her murmur, "Mommy," before tiny hands wrapped around her upper thigh. With that gesture, she made a motion with her finger behind her, one her daughter has seen before. Holly nodded her head against her leg.

"Now you two are…" he didn't finish what he was going to say because as he began to speak Annette took the three remaining steps towards the front door and with her effectively being between the front door and the man in front of her she pushed Holly off her and heard her run.

A horrible grunt noise came from him and he backhanded Annette across the face. She landed against the wall with stars running across her vision. He stormed after Holly. She shook the stars out of her eyes and tried to stand up but she became really dizzy and had to lay back down against the wall. Seconds later she heard stomping coming back in and her whole body tensed. Screaming came with him and she knew Holly hadn't made it.

Terry was dragging a crying, yelling, and kicking Holly in his arms like a rag doll. "No, no, no. Down." She bellowed but he never put her down. He walked back over to the couch and sat down, pulling Holly across his knee. He began smacking her behind with the palm of his hand and now Holly was crying and yelling for a whole other reason. "You will listen and stop running from me. You are mine. You will do what I tell you to from now on." Every sentence he said she got two more slaps across her behind. Annette stood then and screamed so loud she thought glass would break, "Stop!"

His hand stopped mid slap as he turned to her. One hand still holding Holly in place on his lap but didn't need to. Holly had stopped squirming. Annette couldn't see her daughter's face because it was facing the floor but tears were sliding down her cheeks onto the floor. Her heart was breaking into a thousand pieces and she needed to get her daughter out of there.

"Why should I? She needs to learn respect." He sneered at her. His words were like ice in her veins.

"It was my fault. I pushed her towards the door. She didn't do anything wrong." It was true. Annette had indicated for her to run. Only this time it didn't work as it should have.

"Don't worry, a few more and you will get your punishment too." He said. A quirk to his lips before he began his tirade again. One, two, three more smacks of his hand and he placed a sniffling Holly back on her feet in front of him. "Are you going to listen now," he asked. Holly nodded her head silently agreeing. "Come here and give Daddy a kiss sweetness." Annette moved closer to say something but he interjected, "don't move," he put up a hand in her direction, "you will get your turn soon enough."

"I don't," Holly began but he spoke over her, "do you need another spanking for not obeying me?" his words were spoken light but there was a harshness undertone to them. He looked up and down Holly, assessing her as his nostrils flared. At that moment Annette could practically read what he wanted from her little girl and it made her gut lurch.

Holly began to cry all over again. Her red eyes pleading and her hands shaking. Terry just sat there not saying another word, just waiting for her to come to him. As Holly began to move he smiled vehemently to himself. Holly took two steps and Anette was on her feet and moving toward them before Terry could say anything.

She stepped right next to him and placed her hand on his shoulder, pushing the bile rising down her throat. "Baby, I bet Daddy would like a beer. Why don't you go get him a beer?" she said as calmly as she could. What she really wanted to do was punch him in the side of the head and knock him unconscious but she had tried that one before. He was much stronger than she was and he proved that in more ways than one. She just hoped that their sessions on this before would prove to be fruitful now.

Terry's muscles that had tightened under her hand one moment began to relax in the next. "Yea. That sounds good." When she went to follow her Terry placed his arm around her waist, "You stay here. I want some sugar," he said pulling her down on the couch next to him. Holly turned to walk into the kitchen. You could see the obvious relief on the girls' face and it made Annette's chest tighten. At least she could get her daughter out of the house. She didn't care what would happen to her as long as Holly was safe.

He placed a hand under her chin to move her face towards him. His breath smelled rancid as if he hadn't brushed his teeth in months and his body odor wasn't any better. The stench of decay and earth and body odor mixed together to make her head dizzy and the bile started to rise again. She heard the fridge door creak open and shut. Heard a bottle being placed on the counter.

He kissed her then. Held her mouth to his by grabbing the back of her head and holding her firmly in place. His tongue snaked into her mouth forcefully and she didn't move. Didn't part take in the event at all. She sat completely still and just let him do what he was going to do. It was easier not to fight him, she learned that the hard way so long ago that it was just second nature. Although, he could go crazy even without any enticement from her anyway.

He grabbed her knee so hard she was sure she would have a bruise. His finger began to dig into her even over her jeans and she let out a soft cry at the pain. He must have taken it as a noise of pleasure because of what he spoke against her mouth, "Mmmmm. So, good. I knew you liked it." He pulled back to look at her. "I knew I was better than that piece of trash you have been messing around with. He's been giving you a place to stay and food, and all you have to do is warm his bed right." He cleared his throat, "now you can warm mine." They both turned then when there was a small creak. Annette already knew what the noise was and silently smiled to herself.

Terry got up then and walked into the kitchen. He yelled over his shoulder, "stay there." Not listening she stood up ready to run for the door if she needed to. "Where the fuck are you, you little shit." She heard him say and she knew Holly had made it out. *Thank the Lord she was going to be safe*, she thought. She turned to go towards the door and heard him rushing in behind her. "You," was all she heard before she felt something hard hit the back of her head.

She fell to the ground in a daze. Air rushed out of her lungs from the impact of the floor. Her hands splayed out in front of her. She felt hands wrap into her hair and pull her head back, "where did she go?" he hissed into her ear. His knee pressed into her back and the pain had her desperately crying out in agony. He smacked her face into the ground, once, twice, and then pulled her face back up.

"You are going to pay for this." Blood was already running down into her mouth. He must have broken her nose because she heard a crunch. Tears welled up in her eyes and she closed them to will them back. If this was going to be the end, so be it. He pulled her up by her hair and when she stood he placed his other hand at her neck. The strength in him when he squeezed at her throat had her whining against him. "That's it. I love it when you writhe against me. Feel that precious? How hard you have me." She didn't know her side was rubbing into him till he said something and she stilled. The hardness in his pants showing his obvious pleasure at her pain.

In one instant, his hand moved from her neck to slap her across the face, sending another jolt of pain through her. More blood poured from her nose to cover her shirt. He pulled her with him towards the kitchen, "Now to was you up. I don't need you a mess when I finally have my way with you after all this time." When they got to the kitchen he had pulled her head down into the small sink and ran water over her face.

The cleaning he was giving her almost had a waterboarding effect with her mouth and nose directly under the stream of water. She could barely breathe and she was sure every breath she was getting in had water going down her throat. When she was coughing he finally turned the water off. He pulled her up, his hand still in her hair, and yanked her around with him till he found a rag hanging on a cabinet. He harshly wiped her face-off, which also had more blood coming out of her nose. "It will have to do. My, you bleed a lot. We will have to train your body again." He looked her face over and assessed her. "I wish you wouldn't make me hurt you." He said and kissed her again. A harsh peck on the lips that had more pain rushing through her. She whined against his lips. "Shhh, that's a good girl precious," he said.

He began unbuttoning his pants and she knew what was coming, what he wanted from her. She began to cry. Why had she come to the house without Austin? Why did she have to ever get involved with the man standing in front of her? All she wanted right now was to be back in Austin's bed, Holly asleep in her own and the feel of Austin against her. Loving her. But no, she had to come out here and be so stupid. She never wanted to deal with this again and she had thought, for a short time, that she would never have to again. She had been so naive. Now she was paying the price for her choices in life and it was a high price.

She pushed back when she felt his hand loosen on her hair to start to pull down his pants. His hand slipping from her hair she fell back into the kitchen counter. A short stab of pain at the force of it but she turned and began to run towards the front door. She made it halfway before a boot hit the back of her knee and sent her flying to the ground with a thud.

Her hands caught her before her face hit the floor again. "You are going to take it and you are going to like it," he snarled from behind her. The fear she usually felt right about now didn't kick. Instead, she felt a sense of eerie calmness. This was nothing new. She had been through these scenes before. His hand at her back trying to push her down while his pants were down around his thighs. She tried fighting back as she saw the front door crash open.

Her heart leaped to her throat when she saw Austin framed in the doorway. The lowering sun shining behind him as if he was an angle. Terry behind her gave a growl in his throat at the sight before him and the last thing she saw before everything went black was Austin's concerned and angered expression across his face. He was murderous.

Chapter 18

The sight that he walked in on had him ablaze with fury. He had ridden like hell was on his heels the whole way and all but colliding with Gran as he jumped off the horse. She had told him some of what was happening, as she only got bits and pieces from a distraught Holly. He knew he had to make it to the cottage right away. The screams and sounds of struggling when he came up to the porch had him beating down the door. The man leering over Annette had his blood running cold and fire seep up from his stomach.

The sight of her bleeding and hurt had him all but launching himself on the other man but before he could the other man had punched her in the back of the head. Effectively knocking her out. "Move and I'll break her neck," he sneered. His words halted him for a few seconds as the man, he could now assume was Terry from the photos the Sherriff had shown them, began to stand. His pants were down around his knees and the sight of it had the rage that was simmering boiling over. He clenched his fists at his sides and tried to breathe as the other man spoke, "so pretty boy, you have been playing with something that isn't yours," he said as he placed his boot on Annette's unmoving backside. He put more of his weight on her as he leaned toward him, placing a hand on his hip.

Austin heard the sound of cracking like a rib was breaking and it had him wincing inwardly. He knew Annette would be crying out in pain if she wasn't unconscious already. "She isn't yours. Neither of them are. They are not things, they are people." He said through clenched teeth. Holding himself back for

Anette's sake was becoming increasingly more difficult. He wanted to pound the life out of this man. Rip him apart into tiny little pieces and stomp them into the ground but he didn't dare till he knew the other man wouldn't hurt her further.

Terry made a tiny chuckle low in his throat at the statement. Pushing back off her he placed both feet firmly on the floor next to her. The smile he gave was one when you think you have beaten someone in a game of chess, but this game he was playing wasn't over yet. Not by a long shot.

Austin heard the faint sound of hooves in the background behind him. He knew the men wouldn't be far behind. His time at playing fair and nice was running short. He needed to act now before all the men come running in and spook the man. The man in front of him was obviously off-kilter and he didn't want to see what would happen when he was backed into a corner by over a dozen of them.

He knew his moment came when Terry motioned to pull up his pants. He spoke as he moved, "Those two will always be mine. Slaves to whatever I…" he didn't get the rest out since Austin hastily took 3 steps to close the space and landed on the other man. They went crashing into a side table, smashing a lamp before hitting the floor. Austin was on top of him before Terry realized what happened. He got in three punches to the other man's face, breaking his jaw. Terry landed one in Austin's side as he heard some men running up the porch.

"Austin, you in here?" Tony said as the door slammed open again. "In here," yelled another man. Austin was too busy paying attention to the man fighting him on the floor, but when he heard one of the deputies behind him calling for an ambulance on the radio for Annette he must have paused. One moment he was looking over his shoulder for the deputy and the next he heard a gunshot ring out in the room and something ran right by his cheek. He turned around in time to see Terry's shocked expression and a small pistol slide from his hand onto the floor.

It took a moment for Austin to see the dark red stain starting to blossom on his chest since his shirt was already covered in blood. The other man's eyes began to gloss over and soon became lifeless as he slumped back onto the floor. "Nice shot," Cliff said behind him. Austin slowly stood, trying to regain some of his wits before turning around. Tony was placing his gun back in his holster when their gazes locked. "Thanks," he said and Tony just nodded in agreement.

Austin went to Annette then. "Don't move her," officer Ferrell said still sitting next to her on the floor. He nodded, pushing a strand of her hair away from her face. He grimaced at the sight of her broken body sprawled on the floor. He wasn't there when she needed him and he felt like a piece of him died inside. He should have been the one there to protect her and because he didn't want to risk hurting her more he left here there, on the floor. What he really wanted to do was pick her up, cradle her against him and walk her out of here. To feel her body against his, the need to know she was still with him almost debilitating him, but he couldn't. All he could do was sit there and wait. He rubbed her back softly as the others all around him took care of the rest. It was another half hour before he heard the ambulance pull up. The two EMT's came in with a portable stretcher. They politely moved him out of the way and he stood off to the side aching them as they assessed her and took vitals. Another 5 minutes and she was loaded up into the ambulance and headed to the hospital.

He quickly went inside to see Holly and Gran, informing them of what was going on, before running out to his truck and following the sirens of the ambulance. Hugh was already in the house and told him he would help out as much as he could while he was gone. He appreciated the man's word but he got the feeling he had taken a shine to his Gran and would have done it either way. Now his only focus was to make sure his woman was going to make it. She had to. They had just gotten started and he knew he wanted this family with her. She couldn't leave him so soon after coming into his life. It just wasn't fair, so he wouldn't let it happen.

When he got to the hospital, he was told he would have to wait till they got her in a room. Forty minutes later and he was being directed to room 301. Beeping and buzzing from machines greeted him as he entered. The nurse saying the doctor will be in to talk shortly. He took the seat right next to the bed and held her hand. One tear slipped from his eye and down his cheek. He had been resisting them the whole ride there and now they just couldn't be contained. The sight of her limp body hooked up to all those machines, bruises and unconscious was too much for his heart.

"Ahhmmm," someone cleared their throat and it had him looking up. There in the door, a man in a white coat was walking into the room. He extended his hand and Austin took it. "I am Dr. Retaldo," he said, "and you are?"

"Austin McPherson. Annette's boyfriend."

The doctor began flipping through the chart he had in his hand, "OK Mr. McPherson, Mrs. O'Leary shows no signs of a hematoma on the brain, which is a positive. The head wound she sustained however is swollen. It is the reason she is unconscious. When that goes down she should regain consciousness."

"How long before that happens?" He asked watching the doctor who hadn't look at him till that moment. He lifted his gaze to meet his and said blankly, "it is hard to determine these things. It could be in the next minutes or in days. But from the looks of her scans, I would say it should be sooner rather than later." He looked at the chart one more time before placing the chart down on the bottom of the bed.

Austin moved out of the way while the doctor went to look Annette over. Shining a small light into her eyes and feeling for her pulse. He checked her monitors before turning back to him. "Her other injuries will require time to heal. The broken nose will be set in the next hour and we will prescribe her a short supply of pain killers for when she goes home. The bruises will get uglier as they heal but that is only temporary. I will be suggesting she have some outside counseling sessions for the trauma also." He picked up the chart and said, "I will have the nurse come in to start an IV and give her some pain meds," just as he walked out of the room.

Austin went back to sitting in the chair. He caressed her hand not wanting to let go even for a moment. He willed her in his mind to wake up and prayed to anyone who would listen that she would heal from this. He began to drift off but never moved from her side. He fell asleep from exhaustion still clutching her hand at her bedside.

Chapter 19

Pain rippled through every cell in her body when her mind began to work again. Afraid it would cause more pain to open her eyes she kept them shut a little longer. Just listening to the sounds around her for a while and focusing on her breathing. Silence would have been welcome with the ringing in her ears but she was just grateful to be alive that she pushed the irritation back. Beeps and clicks were odd to her but then she realized she must be in a hospital as her memories came flooding back. The struggle with Terry and the pain in her body. She took in a deep breath when she remembered the last thing she saw; Austin's face and she immediately regretted the action. Pain struck in her chest so harsh she gave a tremor and a squeak.

The shift of her body had something move on the sheets surrounding her. What was that? She heard a yawn and then felt a hand on her shoulder. "Baby?" she heard a familiar voice boom. The high pitch sound had her recoiling. "Too loud," she barely got out through her raspy throat. She had never had such a dry throat before. Add that to her rumbling empty stomach and her tired aching body and she was a whirlwind of a mess right now.

"Sorry," he said softer against her ear. "Oh baby, I am so happy you're awake." He held her hand in his bringing it to his chest and leaning over kissed her head. It made tears spring into her eyes and her nose tingle from the swelling of her sinuses. *Oh right, I have a broken nose*, she thought. "Where is Holly?" she needed to know, needed to hear she was ok and safe.

"She is safe back at the ranch. Shhh, you need to rest." When she tried easing up on the pillows he placed a soft hand on her shoulder. His soothing voice against her ear again, "he's gone, sweetheart. For good. He will never touch either of you again." He ran a hand through her hair and his touch was so soft that she relaxed back onto the mattress. Giving in to the sensation of his touch. "I am so sorry for not being there. So very sorry." She could hear the catch in his voice. The tears she assumed he was holding back since she still had yet to open her eyes.

"Stop," she said. "Just don't. None of this…" she had to clear her throat to sound more solid, "None of this is your fault. Don't let his actions be your blame." The sound of him letting out a breath sent shivers down her spine. She couldn't let him take responsibility for what Terry did. There was nothing else he could have done but what he did do.

Before either of them could say anything else she heard a nurse come in, "Is there something you needed in here," her voice was soft with a calming effect that she bet was a pleasure for any of her patients. Annette realized Austin must have buzzed for the nurse when she woke up. "She is awake." She heard the nurse release a rush of air than a pause before feeling cold fingers touch her arm.

She could only assume the woman as checking her vitals as she spoke, "Mrs. O'Leary can you tell me your first name?" Annette answered her after clearing her throat again. "My whole body hurts. It is painful to breathe." Emphasizing with another twitch from trying to take in a breath. "How long have I been here?" the sounds of monitors and lines being moved around after the fingers left her wrist.

No one spoke for so long that she was starting to get worried. Maybe they hadn't heard her. She was just about to ask again when Austin spoke, "It's been six days." That bit of news was a shock. She went to sit up, "What!" she squeaked out but then her body reminded her of her pain and she laid back down.

She could hear more footsteps in the room then followed by more soft voices. A man spoke first, "Mrs. O'Leary, I am Dr. Torrez. I have with me two residences that will be shadowing me in the next few days." He paused and she heard papers shuffling, "How are you feeling right now?"

"My throat is sore," she cleared it once again, "and everything hurts." Trying not to breathe too heavy she focused on the noises from the machines. Click, click, click. Beep, beep, beep. "My ears are ringing too," she added.

"Mmmhmmm," he said a bit nasally she noticed. Maybe he had a cold. "That is understandable. The ringing in your ears is from the head trauma you sustained. It may let up some now that you are awake." He blew his nose. So, her assumptions of him having some kind of cold were more than likely correct. "You have multiple injuries," she felt hands push back the sheet at the bottom of the bed. Cold air flowing over her ankles and feet. "You have contusions or bruises all over," he checked her reflexes by pushing and pulling on her feet, first one then the other. "Good." He said then put the blanket back over her. "You have three cracked ribs which will have to heal on their own. None of them pierced anything so that is a positive sign." He mimicked the same thing he did with her feet but now with her hands. "Your nose was reset," he continued when he was done with her hands, "the breakage, although severe, was easy to fix for a break." He blew his nose again before going on, "you will have bruising around the site for quite some time but it will eventually fade along with the pain."

She felt his fingers feel around her face, testing the skin around her nose and then around the back of her head. She jerked when he hit the spot where she must have been hit. "Sorry," he said pulling back after a few more pokes, "you may have some residual problems like pain or aches with breathing or headaches. If that happens you need to notify your provider. They may want to run some more scans to make sure you don't have any blood clots. Do you understand?" She slowly nodded her head in agreement and regretted the action. The headache got slightly worse and now she was dizzied on top of it.

A hand grasped hers and squeezed. She knew it had to be Austin's so she squeezed it back. A jolt of warmth washed over her knowing he was there. "Mrs. O'Leary, can you open your eyes for me?" Dr. Torrez inquired. When she hesitated, she heard Austin's voice from the other side of her with another squeeze of her hand, "You got this sweetheart. I'm right here." And with that, she pushed past the pain in the back of her eyes to slowly blink them open.

Sunlight assaulted her when she first peaked open. Turning her head some to avert the brightness. She was greeted with Austin's smiling face at her bedside. She smiled at him in relief. He really was there, for her. He had been there all night from the looks of him, maybe even for days. His hair was a mess and he had a stubble of a beard on his usually smooth face. It suited him though just as much as the clean-shaven one did. "You need a shave," she said as the whole room burst out in chuckles. She turned her head in the other direction to see the nurse drawing the curtains to block out some of the sun and a group of men in white coats staring at her. One, in particular, pulled out a tiny light from his side pocket. She recognized him as Dr. Torrez when he spoke, "Now I am just going to shine this light to check your pupils."

The light had her squinting at first because of the sharp pain. However, she was beginning to get used to it by the time he stopped. He turned it off, placed it back in his pocket and then made a note on the pad he had laying on the bed. He stood then turning towards the nurse and residence standing in the room. They talked in hush tones for a few moments then swiveled back in her direction. Her vision was still a bit hazy and she had to blink a few times to get a clearer picture of him.

"Everything looks good from a medical standpoint. We will give it a day and then run your scans again. If they are clear," he sneezed then and pulled out a napkin from his pocket to blow his nose, "sorry about that. If they are clear we will release you the following day as long as nothing else notable happens. For now, just get some rest and let the medication do its job."

"Thank you, doctor," Austin said and extended his hand to the other man. They shook in silent agreement and the white coats all leave the room. Annette looked at the nurse still focusing on the monitors. Her pink floral scrubs did nothing for her figure, which was moderately curvy. She noticed the tired look under her eyes. Her hair was pulled back off her neck and a peeking of a tattoo around her shoulder. The other woman interrupted her grazing eyes with her inquiry, "I hope everything doesn't hurt too bad? At least you will be able to leave soon and we all are so glad your back with us. I know this man probably is," she nodded to Austin as she injected something into her IV line, "He has been here the whole-time barely moving."

Well, that explained the disheveled look of him. The poor man probably has barley slept a wink too. "I am not as bad as I could be I guess." The nurse smiled then, "That's the spirit," she said. "The pain killer I just administered should work pretty quickly to take the edge off. Are you hungry? We can try and get something into your stomach that isn't through an IV now that you're up."

"Some food and something to drink would be amazing. My throat is so dry." She nodded and walked out of the room. "Be right back" she heard her call when she was out the door.

She remembered Austin still held her hand when he squeezed it. Looking down to where their fingers intertwined, she was in awe at it. His masculine touch molded with her feminine one like a perfect fitting glove. She slowly pulled his hand to her mouth, the pain killers must be starting to work because the stabbing sensation in her body was dulling, and when the back of his hand was to her mouth she lingered a kiss there and held it to her cheek. His thumb rubbed up and down her cheek in languid strokes that it soothed her.

His eyes were all glittery with unshed tears when she looked at him again. "I was so afraid I was gonna lose you. I almost can't believe you are here, awake and talking."

"I am too stubborn to leave you. I could have several times by now but I stayed. You think something like this would be any different?" she tried to sound joking but the frown on his face meant he wanted it to be more serious. So, she let out a breath and went on, "Austin…" what could she say? That she was terrified, that she was on edge, that her whole body felt like she had been in a losing MMA match? None of those options would help any and she didn't want to worry him anymore. It was over, now they could both move on, she hoped, together.

Before she could go on, he leaned over and kissed her. His lips so light on her mouth but the stubble around his mouth had her giggling slightly. "That tickles," she said against his mouth. He kissed her once more before moving back. Rubbing his hand over his chin, "sorry. Guess I need a shave."

That moment the nurse came back in with a tray. "Here you go," she placed a tray of red jello, orange juice, cranberry juice, a cup of water, and a green icee down in front of her. "Now try to get something in your belly now. If you can handle this, I will give you a menu to place an order for dinner in a bit." She smiled and adjusted the tray and bed so she was up and sitting comfortably. Austin was hovering around the side of the bed looking so uncomfortable for a moment she wanted to pull him in close.

Annette nodded in agreement. "Now," the nurse continued, "you will be getting tired from the medicine to try to get as much in as you can before you rest. I want to make sure your tummy gets something in it. Now I'll leave you to it. Buzz me if you need anything." With that last statement, she turned on her heel and walked back out of the room.

Annette's stomach growled but her eyes were starting to get relaxed. Her head felt like it was getting heavier too. Austin must have noticed because he leaned over and kissed her head again. "I am going to go home, shower and change. I'll bring Holly and Gran by this evening if you want visitors? Or I can just swing by on my own?" He questioned. She knew even if she said no to one or both of those options, she would still have visitors regardless and it made her smile to herself. She picked up the cup of cranberry juice and sipped. Groaning at the sear joy of taste and liquid in her mouth and down her throat.

Meeting his eyes, "I would like as much company that wants to come." She replied. He smiled, brushed his lips against hers and put his forehead to hers, "you may regret those words," a sparkle light his eyes. He pulled back, gave a slight wave and hesitated a moment before walking out the door. Annette sat there a few seconds before drinking the rest of her cranberry juice and eating the jello and ice. She drifted off to sleep in a sitting position a short while later and felt the bed being laid back for her but not motivated enough to open her eyes. She heard the nurse go "Shhhh. Relax." Before she did just that and drifted off into sleep.

****

The last two days had gone in a blur. Annette woke to tons of people filling her room. They were all there to welcome her back to the land of awareness now that she was awake. The Sherriff got her statement but only after she ate her breakfast, per the nurse's instructions. Austin never left her side. She wasn't sure if it was to make her comfortable or if it was to find out exactly what happened himself. She figured it was a bit of both. Sherriff Townsend informed both of them about everything they found at Terry's camping site. They are keeping everything for evidence and Annette didn't mind one bit after learning about the photos he took. The information had sent chills down her spine. Sherriff Townsend had gotten an odd look on his face just before he asked her some questions that made her uneasy.

"I have to ask but has Terry ever done anything to your daughter?" His expression never wavered and it sent more chills up and down her spine. She felt Austin rub her shoulder. She looked back and forth between both men before she found her voice.

When she did answer it was so soft both men leaned in a bit to hear. "No," her eyes dropped to her hands that were cradled together in her lap, "not that he didn't try to. He was a twisted man. I am just sorry I didn't see it sooner." Her head snapped up at the sharp intake of breath from Austin. He looked regretful but she didn't know what he had to be regretful of. None of this was his fault.

Tony sighed loudly before he started to explain, "we found two notebooks at the site with the photos. Some of the scribblings were of dates and what I assume was him taking notes of whatever you had been doing." He cleared his throat and shuffled his hat in his hands. The look in his eyes began to soften but his jaw seemed very taunt. The vein in his neck seemed more pronounced all of a sudden.

"Get it out," Austin said through clenched teeth. His stroking of her shoulder had stopped.

"The rest was filled with what he called his 'To-Do Wish List' and it was hard to get through, let me tell you." Tony looked increasingly uncomfortable, "one of the deputies got sick while reading some of it. It went into great detail about what he was going to do to Holly and you when he got you back. Some of it was sexual too. I won't go into detail because it is irrelevant now that he is gone but I just wanted to make sure if anything had ever happened."

Annette had tears in her eyes that she didn't bother to wipe away. Austin walked over to the window and kicked the radiator while slamming his palms on both sides of the frame. No one spoke for a long while. Tears had slipped down her cheeks and she didn't realize he was there till Austin began wiping them away. He tilted her chin up towards him and kissed her lightly.

"Well, like I said he's gone so it doesn't matter. We are all just glad of that. So, I am going to get going." He placed his hat back on his head, "Tony," she said, "I have a notebook of notes on incidents and places we were at. It might help clear up some of the timelines if you would like it. I won't be needing it anymore." He nodded his head.

"That would be nice. When you have time, you can drop it off or I can stop by and pick it up." He nodded again tilting his head. He turned and walked out of the room.

Annette had told Austin where her notebook was so he could drop it off later. Carolynn and her daughter had come the night before that but they also came back with Austin bright and early in the morning. Every single one of the men that came by for the search party had shown up at the hospital too.

Some with their wives who all brought some sort of edible.

The food was piling up that Carolynn said her fridge and freezer back at the ranch was already full. When the day arrived for her to leave the hospital Austin had to make two trips for all the flowers and extra food that was in her room. She giggled in the truck at the memory of his flustered face. He wasn't sure if he was going to make everything fit but he was determined not to make the trip a third time just to fetch her. He had said he "didn't want to waste over an hour each way just to haul everything but the one thing he wanted." He was referring to her and heat rushed to her cheeks at his brashness. He had been so sincere but adorable about it.

When they were leaving, he would not let her walk at all. After the nurses wheeled her out, a standard procedure of every patient, he plucked her out of the chair and sat her in the truck. She protested at first stating she could walk herself, but he just put a hand up and told her not to bother arguing. That was the end of that in his mind. Now she was sitting in the truck, staring out at the landscape going by.

This kind of reminded her of the first time she rolled into this town. It was dark outside and although she knew there was nothing but farms and fields around her now, you still couldn't see very far. The light of the moon was barely registering because of how dark it was. At least this time around it wasn't raining. A lot has happened in the time she pulled up in her old car in front of a diner and had Carolynn waltz into their life.

They both had a stable home, her daughter actually had things to call her own, they had food regularly, not having to run or even worry about running, and they now had a family. Terry was no longer a problem and hopefully, soon she would get him out of her mind completely. Every night in the hospital was filled with nightmares of him and sometimes during the day too. She noticed how less frequent she had them while she had been at the ranch. Her defenses had come down some and she had become comfortable.

She decided it suited her. It suited both of them. Holly had blossomed while they had been there, taking to Carolynn and Austin so easily. Her heart sang every time she saw them with her. The smiles and laughter that accompanied their presence filled her heart with so much joy it almost hurt. She used to worry about her or Holly getting too attached to anyone or any place. The inevitable would happen and they would have to leave it all behind. But now, there is hope. Hope for a future with more than pain, worry, and heartache – and it had her a bundle of nerves at times. She didn't know what was next but this time it was exciting not a feeling of doom.

She turned to Austin. Peering at him through the darkness with only the light glow of the dashboard she could see the faint wrinkles by his eyes. She saw his relaxed grip on the steering wheel. He had one arm on the wheel and the other on the back of the bucket seat like he was waiting for her to move closer. He hadn't said one word the whole time they drove. He must have been in deep in thought like she was, she deduced.

With his arm not moving from the back of the seat she decided to slide closer to him. She unbuckled and skootched over, leaning her head against partially against his shoulder and partially against his chest. He was so warm, soft and hard all at once. His arm left the seat and rested around her. He pulled her close to his side and turned to kiss the top of her head before laying his cheek on top of hers. She sighed at the contact of him. His scent swirling around her senses and making her heart skip a beat. This is where she was meant to be and she was never going to let it go.

When they pulled onto the driveway, he lifted his head. "Everyone will probably be asleep. It is after midnight. They sure kept you till the last minute but never mind that. You are home now and safe. We will get you inside and in bed. Figure out the rest in the morning." She knew he was rambling and she guessed it was because he still couldn't believe she was finally back. The way he touched her after waking up in the hospital she sensed it was to constantly make sure she was real, that this was real, and she couldn't fault him for it. If it had been him in the hospital, she would have lost it too.

"OK." He stopped the truck in front of the porch steps and shifted towards her. The length of time they stared at each other seemed to go on for hours but it could only have been a few minutes. She didn't know what to say and he looked like he might have been fighting himself to get out what he wanted, so she just waited. Giving him time to work it out in his head. When he finally started to speak it was so sudden that she jumped in her seat.

"I wasn't there when you needed me." He noticed her jump and he reached out a hand to her cheek, "Are you ok?" She nodded and waited for him to go on. "I have never been so scared as when I saw him on top of you and your body on the floor." He looked out the window, his hand falling from her face and he placed both of them on the steering wheel. "I have never loved someone as much as I love you and Holly. I promise to be there for you both forever." He turned his head to look at her then, "I can't go through that ever again. I know that bastard is gone and he can't hurt you now but I don't want to ever see you or Holly hurt or scared like that about anything ever again." He took in a breath since he didn't breathe through any of that. She just stared at him. All his words wrapping around her in a hug. "You are a part of this family; you are my family and I will always put family first. I just need to know if what happened will have you leaving because if you leave, I will follow you. You can't get away from me now."

Without warning and before she was able to get out a sound, he turned to her, took her face in his hands and kissed her. His tongue outlined her bottom lip before plunging into her mouth. Nothing about this kiss was timid or soft. This kiss was about need, desire, and promises. She wasn't sure if she moaned or if he did. Their bodies tried to get closer but it was awkward in the cab of the truck. He moved his hands down to cup her breast over her shirt and the other wound around her back. She moved her hands to wrap around his neck. Their tongues danced and swirled together.

Abruptly he pulled back leaving them both panting. Taking in a few deep breaths had her chest aching but she spoke through it, "I love you too and we are not going anywhere." The radiant smile he gave her had her body warming again. He kissed her lightly and quickly this time before opening the truck door. He got out and quickly moved to her side. He lifted her duffle bag over his shoulder and picked her up. She relaxed into him while he cradled her against his muscled chest. She could feel the hardness of him through his shirt. His breath came out in pants as he took the steps two at a time. He dropped the duffle bag when he came inside the door. It hit the bench and fell to the floor. Making noise in its wake.

"Shhhh," she said. "You will wake the house." He crinkled up his nose and she found another face of his she adored. "I'm hungry. Can we eat?"

"No"

"But I haven't eaten in hours." She protested.

"I told you I was taking you to bed." He walked down the hallway towards the stairs. Not letting her down as he started up them.

"You know the doctor said no strenuous activity." She wiggled her eyebrows at him. He looked down at her when he reached the top and looked at her briefly. "I know," he replied.

"Well, I am starving. I need to eat." He opened his bedroom door and lightly placed her on the bed. Standing and working his shirt off his torso.

"Oh, I know but I am hungry too, just not for food right now. And sweetheart, this isn't strenuous at all. For either of us." He gave a sly smile and dropped his shirt to the floor. The look on his face didn't mask the naughty thoughts he was having in the least.

Epilogue

These past three months have felt like her whole life has been revamped. No more threats to worry about has been amazing for all of them. Austin has been so attentive and has taken care of them so well that sometimes she wonders how she deserved such a man. The concept was so foreign to her that she had to combat the awkward feeling of being a burden. Although Austin keeps assuring her it was his pleasure to do it, she just couldn't help it sometimes. Hopefully one day she just would accept it as so, but until then she would work on it.

Since that night Austin took it upon himself to move them back into the main house and with that, he had moved her things into his room. Holly never minded because she liked being close to everyone and that in turn made Annette more comfortable too. She had just completed another book and sent it off to her editor, whim said it was the best she had ever written. It was about a girl on the run from her ex, which everyone who knew what happened to them could guess the ending. Turns out taking inspiration from real life sometimes made for great publishing.

Now she was outside with Austin waiting for the school bus. It was Holly's first day and she knew that she was way more nervous for her daughter then her daughter was. Holly couldn't wait to go to school today. She woke up way too early this morning and pulled out all of her toys trying to shove each one in her backpack to show everyone at school. She and Austin both had to gently explain that she couldn't take her toys to school. Holly was disappointed she couldn't bring her birthday toys in to show everyone.

She had just turned four a month ago and after having Carolynn talking her ear off, they both came to the conclusion it was time to put her in kindergarten.

Austin placed an arm around her as they watched the bus coming up the long drive and whispered in her ear as if he had been reading her thoughts, "Calm down. She will have done fine today. I bet she is so excited when she comes off the bus." He gave her shoulder a squeeze before he let his arm drop as the bus pulled up in front of them.

The smiling bus driver greeted them as the doors opened. They both said hi to her and waved just before an elated Holly bounced down the stairs and jumped into his arms.

She started speaking just as the bus drove away, "Mommy! Daddy! I went to school! I drove a bus!" Holly had started calling Austin daddy while she was in the hospital. She supposed it was because of her daughter that he embodied what a dad should be. A protector and caregiver. Either that or she just wanted a family and she saw one with them. All of them. Austin and she had a long conversation about what it meant to allow Holly to call him that and that same discussion also lead to what they were together.

That was when they agreed to give this relationship a go. She hadn't been in a serious relationship as boyfriend and girlfriend in over a decade. So, this was new to her and she constantly felt like she needed a refresher course. According to Austin, she was doing fine and he wouldn't have her any other way. Sometimes they talked about marriage, settling down and future plans but she was not sure if it would become a reality. She was so used to living in the now that planning was not something that came easily to her. So, she let him focus on that topic.

Holly and Austin were still talking next to her and it pulled her back to what was going on around her. "... made it great!" he said and she shook her head. "What was that?" she asked.

"Our munchkin gave me a picture she made of all of us," he said holding it out to her. She just noticed he had a purple paper in his hand of stick figures standing side by side. Two tall with one small one in the center drawn in red. They all were smiling. On top, it said 'My Family' and underneath it said 'daddy, mommy and me'. It had tears creeping into her eyes. Austin continued as she looked at it. "I told her she made this picture great." Holly beamed at them over her drawing. Holly saw Carolynn come out onto the front porch and wriggled down from his arms. She ran up the steps to show Carolynn her drawing, hearing the other woman "Ooo" and "Ahh" over the picture.

She turned to look at Austin when she heard him clear his throat. He looked nervous when he spoke and that had her guard up. "I know thanksgiving is about three months away and I was wondering how you would feel about having a November or December wedding." It took a few minutes to register what he was saying. When the words began to sink in her stomach started doing little flip flops at the realization. "What?" was all she could get out. Her mouth had gone dry and she had to lick her lips. He sank down to one knee and pulled out a red velvet box from his pocket.

"Everyone will already be here. Thanksgiving is a big deal for our family and neighbors. Two birds and one stone." He replied looking up at her.

"Are you asking me what I think you're asking me?"

So much hope-filled his eyes that it made her chest ache. How could she deny this man? The man who had lassoed her heart already and had shown her what it means to feel loved. Carolynn chimed in from the porch, "Honey you'd better take that man before someone else snatches him up. We don't have all day." Annette giggled without looking at the other woman. Her eyes were glued to Austin's.

"Sweetheart." He rasped, "Annette O'Leary, would you do me the greatest honor," he opened the box to show a rose gold infinity band of diamonds, "and become Mrs. McPherson?" He began to pull the ring out of the box.

"Do we have to wait that long?" she asked realizing she didn't want to. He let out the breath she guessed he must have been holding and gave a small chuckle. Relief spread across his features and a half-smile quirked the corner of his mouth.

"Gran would like something for the whole family and I don't think either of us wants to disappoint her. But if you want to, we can go down to the courthouse tomorrow." She was already shaking her head. She knew she couldn't do that to Carolynn. "You are right. We can't disappoint Gran. Just promise me it will be simple."

He placed the ring on her finger and kissed her as he stood. This kiss was a promise all on its own. Deep and passionate. It took her breath away and felt like they had been kissing there for hours when in reality it was only a minute or two.

"Sweetheart I will promise you anything you want if it means getting you to take my hand and last name." He sighed against her lips. He pulled her to him. He pressed her so hard against him that it took the air out of her for a moment. "Now you will be able to meet the rest of the family." She pulled her head back enough to look up at him. "Will they like me?" she felt a bit nervous at meeting these people that meant so much to him. He nodded his head at her and placed a kiss to her forehead. "They will adore you."

Holly ran up to them and hugged their legs. "Can we eat?" she asked before pulling back and running back up the stairs. Carolynn and Holly both went back inside the house leaving Austin and Annette smiling after her.

He took her hand in his and nudged her towards the door. "I think our daughter wants food." With her fingers entwined in his, she let him lead her towards the front door. Her world felt so complete at that moment that she wished she could bottle it up. She realized she would need to buy a camera to take pictures of all the memories she wished to never forget. Starting with her new family that she was never going to let go of. No more running for her, and that was a promise she would always keep.

The End

If you enjoyed this first installment, pick up book two **Their Somewhere Safe,** the next installment of The Rayne Falls Rach Series. Till next time remember....
"You can't have history without a story in it."

Preview
Their Somewhere Safe

Prologue
"You sure you want to drive yourself? My offer still stands to fly with me?" Reed yelled from the bathroom. His oldest brother always liked to arrive in style anywhere he went. "No, I'm good. I have been flying around so much I'd rather stick to the ground for a while." Kent replied. He had just gotten back from his second tour; this one was in Egypt and he took a month's leave to attend Austin's wedding. His younger brother was getting married to Annette, a mother of a little girl. From what he understood she had a lot of problems with her ex-husband, the birth father of her little girl, and domestic abuse. It all came to a head when he attempted to harm both of them and was shot dead. Now Austin has stepped up and is officially adopting the little girl, who already calls him Daddy and marrying the woman he loves in nine days.

The fridge door slammed shut hard when he used his foot to close it after grabbing a cold one and a package of pepperoni. It must have been louder than he thought when he heard his brother again, "Don't be breaking shit in my house!" He chuckled opening the package and taking a handful into his mouth. The bold flavor exploding over his tongue had his mouthwatering. It was still early, around seven in the morning but he planned on getting a move on since it was a 33-hour drive and he wasn't sure yet if he planned on driving the whole way or if he was getting a hotel for a break. Also, he planned to make a few stops along the way. Finishing his snack and his drink, he walked over to the window and gazed out at the sprawling city below. Reed lived in a penthouse condo overlooking central park in Manhattan. His brother had money and had no problem spending it on the finer things. He couldn't blame him though. This view was amazing and he knew he would never get tired of looking at it. It was just everything surrounding it that had him homesick.

Nothing but skyscrapers and tall buildings surrounded the green patch of land. People that looked like ants roamed around everywhere and the slight fog of the air had his heart aching for open land and blue sky. He missed his military family and their banter but his heart was also torn towards his home town. He left to serve his country with his friend, Jason, who died in a desert from an assault on their convoy. Jason had thrown himself in front of him and another soldier and got hit in the chest. The bullet went through him and hit Kent in the collar bone. It took their medic team 2 hours to retrieve the bullet from the bone. He still had pain from it every once in awhile, but he would never get over the loss of his friend. The bullet severed a coronary artery right near Jason's heart and he bled out internally before the medic team had shown.

"Bro, you listening to me," snapping of Reed's fingers in his face had Kent turning his head to his brother. Confused for a moment, Kent shook his head to bring him back from his memories. After the fog in his head cleared enough, "what is it?" His tone coming out a bit harsher than he meant it to but if Reed noticed he didn't say anything.

"Man, where was your head at?" His older brother ran a hand over the short stubble of a beard on his chin. Reed had started to show some signs of greying, which Kent teased him for when he got back but in all honesty, it suited his brother. Reed had always been the more mature one out of all three of them.

"Nowhere," Kent replied. Not wanting to get into it right now. Shrugging, Reed turned and went to the kitchen Island. Kent watched as he lifted a glass of tea and took a sip. *When had he gotten that*, Kent wondered? He must have really been out of it not to hear the fridge.

Reed spoke between drinks, "I am still surprised you don't have a date to this thing lined up. You could always pick one up on the way down there I'm sure." He knew Reed was teasing him to make light of everything and he appreciated it. Joining Reed at the island, Kent rolled out his shoulders.

"I have enough of my own problems. I don't need to add in someone else's right now. Besides, you can be my date." He gave his brother a big smile, "remember when you pick me up, I don't like flowers, I prefer beer and I don't put out on the first date." His brother went to laugh as he was drinking and started hacking. Kent slapped him on the back a few times till he caught his breath. They both stood there for a few minutes just chuckling. When they caught their breath Reed spoke, "and I always thought you were easy." Reed moved to place his cup in the dishwasher and he turned to go to his room to grab his bags. Kent yelled over his shoulder, "I'm playing hard to get." He heard Reed's laugh follow him down the hall.

Packing wasn't hard since he just got to Reed's four days ago and hadn't even unpacked. He left all his military gear in his locker on base and only brought two duffle bags and a large camping style backpack. He didn't want to mention it to his brother but he really wanted the drive just to think and get his mind straight before he was around everyone. Reed usually stayed to himself and didn't ask too many questions which he was grateful for since he didn't want to talk about anything yet. Kent knew he wouldn't know where to start even if Reed did ask. Thankfully his brother wasn't the nosey or inquisitive type.

"When I get there after my meetings we will have to go get you a proper suit. I can't have my date looking like a hobo." Reed slapped him on the back as he placed his things in front of the door. He would have fallen headfirst into the door if he hadn't put his hand up to catch himself.

"I owe you for that later," Kent brushed his jeans when he got up. His hand ran over his freshly cut military crop. Stubble was already growing on his chin again and he knew he would need another shave again by tomorrow. Usually, he had to do it once a day it grew so fast.

He met Reed's eyes, which wasn't hard to do since they were maybe two inches or so difference in height, Kent being the taller of the two. "When don't you owe me, man," Reed replied with a shit-eating grin. "Don't forget Beauty when you leave," his brother tossed him his car keys. "I just had the oil changed again last week. She should be good for a while." Kent fingered the keys in his palms.

The keys felt so odd in his hands. "Thanks for watching her man."

"Anytime man. Hopefully, you get to play with her for a while." Reed slapped him on the back one last time and pulled him in for a brief hug before letting him go. Walking around him he held the door open. Kent slung the backpack over his shoulder, picked up the other two bags and patted his pocket, making sure his wallet was in there. "See ya in a few days, man." He said before walking to the elevator. He got in when the door clicked open and pressed the button for the garage. Excited about seeing Beauty again, he all but hopped out of the elevator when it slid open. A horn honked and lights flashed as he hit the locator button on the keychain.

Beauty was a black Dodge Charger with black rims and matching black interior. He had red undercarriage lights installed and a new exhaust the last time he was home two years ago. He had Reed install a new Hemi engine into her while he was away in preparation for his return. Seeing her now in all her glory he could not lie, he had a semi hardon just from the sight of her. He pushed the button to open the trunk and stored his bags in it. He let out a grunt as the weight of the backpack eased off his sore shoulder and into the trunk before closing it. Slowly Kent slid his hand over the exterior. Beauty felt smooth as he made his way to the driver's side door.

Once inside he grabbed the steering wheel and eased back in the seat. Breathing in the smell of leather, gas, and metal had his body relaxing. He missed this. Adjusting his rearview mirror and side mirrors before he put the stick in reverse, pulling out of the garage. The sun was already set high in the sky but it didn't stop the crisp of the air making fog on the windshield. The dark black tint on the windows and windshield helped with the brightness but he was still putting on his sunglass anyway. The sound of the engine had his heart rate picking up and his mood felt lighter with every mile closer that he got to home.